The Twin Flame Codes

A Novel

Shoena Helen Harris

The Twin Flame Codes

Cover designed by D. Hanna

ISBN: 978-1-965142-55-4 (Paperback)
ISBN: 978-1-965142-56-1 (Hardback)
LCCN: 2025917713

Quill Hawk Publishing
Edmond, Oklahoma

Table of Contents

Author's Note

This story comes from my 35 years of experience as a student of spiritual mysteries. My teachers helped me to learn the codes that structure our lives. The codes are from higher planes of existence that many of us once called home. I have woven many of those codes into this story. They are a subtle database that I created for this reality. It is available for any reader who chooses to receive it. After my personal immaculate conception, Mother Mary told me that this was what she experienced, but it was rejected because humanity wasn't ready for an internal rebirth: "My journey led me to discover the inner door of the heart. My son and I have been knocking on many heart doors for over 2,000 years now, but many have not recognized my presence in them. We've been shining the heart's light on the treasure chest within their body, encouraging them to find it. *Go inside,* I would whisper. *Explore it and feel me, find me in you.* It started a movement of awareness to find someone to love, to procreate from love rather than from lustful, animal instincts. *Find unconditional love* was my directive, *get out of judgment*, but our story was externalized and, therefore, not understood."

"Dear, you are bringing in the next evolutionary leap for mankind," she told me. That old story that we've been talking about as an historical event must be turned into an internal awakening if we are to take the physical body through its transformation process. We must reclaim our power. We must understand that our genes were severely altered from their original design as a divine BEING of soul and spirit. The soul was split apart by dark, off-planet entities who manipulated the body and then called it their own creation. They hijacked the creation of Mother Earth out of her own body. My mission is to redeem our beloved body so that it can continue its original journey of self-discovery as a Divine Source Creator, the living offspring of Mother Sophia and Father Sun, not a corrupt body programmed to live in fear.

This series is loaded with power-packed encodings to repair and restore our original source connection at a biological level, reconnecting our universal, divine genetics to our current physical genetics and allowing, through our heart spark, to reignite the half that has been dormant and disconnected. Reunite the two halves to Wholeness. From here, your inner healer can assist the body to remember what it once was and what it once knew. But to do this you must use a key, unlock your heart's soul door, and go back inside. This activates the lost and forgotten codes that've been stored and locked away in your heart's treasure chest. Wake up and know that you already possess the key. Claim it. Reach deep into that hidden pocket and retrieve it. The codes in my story will unlock a sequence of tumblers when you are ready. I am the prototype for transformation into the Divine Human. From this spark chamber, we can reverse-engineer the harmful side of what they did. We must restore our multi-dimensional, universal, spiritual genetic gateway, which was severed from the heart's flame, and reopen it. The answers to all of our searching questions have always been within us. Open your emerald door and retrieve what's yours.

1. A Cry for Help

"What was that?" Abrum stopped dead in his tracks. It sounded faint, far off, like a distress call. He stood frozen, waiting to see if it repeated. Slowly crouching to the ground, he tried to hone in on the direction it came from. The sun would be setting soon, and the density of this part of the forest meant he would have to be careful when he heard another cry for help. Could there really be someone else in these remote woods? "Hmm, no more distress calls. Why?' Remembering his first experience in these woods, he decided to relax and wait on an old log. He understood far too well what that person might be going through. He sat there remembering his mother and why he came here in the first place. An old, familiar ache moved through him.

Mother, he said to himself, *I miss you.* His love for her filled his aching heart. After his father died, she never remarried. The two of them became extremely close. She taught him all of the history and traditions of her family that had been passed down to her. When he left on this journey, she could no longer get out of bed, but she insisted that he go and that his uncle would take care of her. He closed his eyes and searched for her in his memory. He could feel her presence inside, like he always did, and he smiled. His visit triggered her awareness of him.

Son ... Son, I'm here. I feel you wondering about me. They could still communicate despite the distance that separated them. *You'll know when I cross over because I will visit you first, I promise. Don't worry about me. I'm okay, just as I know you'll be okay when I leave this plane. I've completed what I came to do, and I have faith that you will, too.*

A part of himself still felt like a small child, still needing his mother to protect him. As he pondered that feeling, he assured himself he would be okay. He didn't want to lose her, and he still had to know when she exited her body, but he was ready to live his own life. She'd taught him well. He would miss her deeply, but he already felt his path opening up for him from these first few days on the road. She would always be with him in his heart. He heard her reassuring voice telling him the same thing.

We share a sacred heart connection that lasts forever. Even when I leave this body, I'll be there with you in the new life you've started. Don't ever forget that. I'll be there. I see it. This is your destiny. I love you always. You are my heart, Abe. Now, go do what you have to do. I'll be okay.

He felt her love for him. A strong pang of emotion hit him at the thought of her impending death. He placed his palms over his heart to release the emotion and replace it with unconditional love. A big smile spread across his face.

Mother, I feel you. I love you.

He felt his body accepting her love. It helped him to accept her approaching departure. He held her in his heart as he remembered the dream that joyfully followed her throughout her life. It would replay itself every full moon. She always stood next to a clear mountain stream with a group of young people, the sun just coming up. Sometimes she would morph into a tree, a bird, an animal, an elemental being, always something different. Then she would speak to the students in the language of that being, and they would hear what it was like to live in that form.

It became his dream as well as hers because he heard it so many times. She told their whole family. Over the years, he grew to understand that this was her way to pass on the family roots that connected them to the planet. Whenever any of them needed some new information, her guidance delivered it in a dream.

He greatly admired her gift as a seer. Because of her, he learned to become a dream walker, too. She also mastered the skill of astral traveling, navigating in and out of multiple planes. Each generation passed down their seer-ship abilities, keeping the family legacy alive. She told him often that it was their job, their mission, to respect and honor their intuitive gifts and keep them alive for generations to come.

I've seen it — a time when people will completely lose their inner guidance and wander through life like lost sheep, afraid of everything. I will not allow that in my family! Abe, I know your purpose in life because I, like my mother, made the same decree: any child who comes through my womb will carry on our abilities, maintaining a devoted channel for souls to keep their source connection alive. We believed in it so strongly that we mothers always chose the souls that we birthed. You are here to complete the prophecies for the next generation, just like it's been done since we left Zathera. It's our way of life.

He could feel the ring of truth in his gut.

As he sat in silence, a memory came back of one of his mother's repeated dream scenarios. It pertained to a legend about an ancient tree. In many of her dreams, the tree would take on a personality and magically talk to her.

When you dream dimensionally, anything is possible, she would say.

He wondered how the tree saga might eventually play out. Among all of his mother's visions and dreams, the tree spoke the most to him because he also had strange dreams concerning the "tree people," as he called them. He didn't have it all figured out, but it always seemed to be looming in the background of his awareness, a constant, overshadowing presence.

After coming here, that same eerie presence grew even stronger. He wondered what it all meant. He felt he could speak to them, but he still couldn't understand their message. He marveled at how big these trees were. They made him feel as tiny as an ant.

***

He brought his awareness back to the present. He listened intently for the slightest sound. All quiet, but he sensed a presence, different from his mother. He felt a warning signal in his gut. *It must be coming from whoever is out there.* Sure enough, off in the distance, he heard another stressful cry for help. He honed in on the direction more clearly this time. He heard two more cries. He jumped up, grabbed his pack, and headed in the direction of the sound. He yelled, "Hello, I'm coming, keep calling."

He found an animal trail, making it easier for him to run. He drew closer. The voice sounded feminine. *What is a girl doing out here?* Her screams cut deep inside him. He put one hand over his heart to protect himself.

Whoa, calm yourself. Getting excited isn't going to help. He couldn't be sure if his heavy breathing was just from running or also because of his concern for her. The thought of finding someone else here impacted him more than he imagined it might.

Breathe your centering breath, he reminded himself, *and stay focused. I have to find her first. I'm aware of some connection here, but that can wait.*

As he rounded a thick stand of brush, he recognized the place. Several days earlier, he found a wild plum thicket just to the north. He made a mental note to come back in a few days when the fruit grew ripe. Like everything else here, it was big.

There is some strange magic here. Everything is thriving like I've never seen anywhere else.

As he made his way through the underbrush, he realized she must be calling from a hole because her voice sounded muffled and bounced around as if in a cave.

"I'm down here!" she screamed.

The brush suddenly gave way to a gaping sinkhole. He gingerly tested his footing and leaned over the edge. She lay there, propped up against a boulder.

"Hang on." I'll get you."

A bloody stain ran down the side of her head. "My leg hurts. I can't stand up." She put her hand on her belly with a sense of urgency.

That's odd, he thought. *She doesn't seem to have any injury there. I'll have to check on that later.* "You're going to be okay. I'm coming." A couple of big trees had fallen across the hole, so he used those to lower himself down. He struggled to keep his footing amid all of the rocks. "Okay, I'm here." Dried blood crusted her face from the head wound. "Let's see your leg." He gingerly touched her leg and examined it carefully. "It looks like you've just sprained your ankle. Do you hurt anywhere else?"

She shook her head. "No."

"Well, let's get you out of here." He worked with wood at home, giving him plenty of strength, but the depth of the hole made it difficult to just lift her out. He retrieved his knife from his backpack to cut a couple of branches. With those and his bedroll, he created a sling, but could he tie it all together? He rifled through her backpack and found some thongs that tied onto her ankle with long shoelaces. With these, he completed the sling. He gently picked her up and put her into the sling. He tied her into it using one of his long-sleeved shirts. With care and using all of his strength, he propped her up against one of the trees and slowly inched her out of the hole.

He laid her down and removed all of the bindings. By this time, she had slipped into unconsciousness. He took a closer look at her leg. Nothing appeared to be broken. The gash in her forehead needed cleaning, but it would heal. He worried about a possible concussion. He sat down beside her to catch his breath. He lay on the ground to soak up some earth energy. He visualized an energetic tail that he could sink deep into the ground. He took deep breaths, projecting his heart forces down through his invisible tail. His mother taught him that this could keep his body's battery charged throughout the day. Once he felt the familiar link-up, he drew the girl into his regenerating flow. After several minutes, he felt his body re-energized enough to figure out what to do next.

He sent a subliminal message to activate more of her healing forces through his conscious intent, even though he couldn't be sure of the right timing. Did she have enough awareness to link herself up while she waited for help? She lay unconscious, so he decided to do it for her. He aligned with her breathing rhythm and felt the two of them connect. They linked so quickly, he realized she must use this same practice. A momentary excitement pulsed through him: *She's not a foreigner lost in the woods. She's traveling a sacred path to find her roots, just like me!* He smiled and returned to his focus to her healing.

The sun settled down among the trees. The forest would soon be dark. He didn't have time to get her back to the old dwellings he'd found. He remembered finding a plush carpet of thick grass next to a nearby creek, a perfect place to camp for the night.

He picked her up. Once he reached the spot, he laid her down gently and began to unroll a couple of thick, woolen blankets, neatly woven together with red and brown threads, from her backpack. Someone put a lot of love into them. He doubled one over, put it on the green grass, and laid her on it. She looked beautiful despite the cut. He sensed an inner beauty and joy in her biofield. *Stop it,*" he reminded himself. *"Get back to work. You've got a lot to get done before it gets even darker."*

He filled up their water jugs and gathered some firewood. The warmth would help to relieve her shock. The sparks from his flint ignited some dry leaves. He carefully added small twigs, then some larger ones. Soon, the fire crackled brightly, and he turned to get her cleaned up. She moaned and put her hand to her head. She slowly opened her eyes and gave him a blank stare.

"Don't worry. You're safe," he said. You fell into a hole, but you're okay now. I lifted you out. Do you remember anything?"

"A little," she moaned. "Not much, really."

"Just lie still. You've got a nasty cut on your head. I'm going to clean it up and look at your ankle. I'll try not to hurt you, but I have to get your shoe off." He loosened the leather straps and slowly pulled it off. "It's bruised and swollen. You're going to have to stay off of it for a while. I'll find something to wrap it."

"There's some stuff in my bag," she whispered.

He started digging through her backpack. "You've got herbs," he said. "When I first found you, you rubbed at your belly as if you were in pain. Did you hurt yourself there?"

"No, it's fine." She put her hand on her belly, then quickly pulled it off. "Can I see the herbs, please?" She fumbled through them and handed some to him. "These will make a poultice."

He took the herbs and a pot that she had, dipped some water from the creek, and put it next to the fire to soak the poultice.

"OK, let's take a look at your head." The bleeding stopped, so he dipped a cloth in the creek and cleaned off as much of the dried blood as he could. A gash ran along the right side of her head above her ear. "We need something to wrap around this." He found what he needed among her things. "You should be good for now. You're sure you have no pain in your stomach or abdomen?"

"No, it's fine. Thank you."

"Can you eat something?" he asked.

She nodded. "I have a little bread and some dried fruit and veggies."

"Great. I can make us a soup." When it was ready, he helped her to take a few bites.

"That's enough," she said and laid back down. She closed her eyes, and he soon heard her rhythmic sleep breathing. He spotted her Bogo bag of moonstones and placed them around her. He paid respect to the gemstones and asked for permission to use them to help her. Sensing approval, he set up a grid around her body. He took the bag with the remaining stones and placed it on her chest over her heart. He found a cedar stick to smudge the stone grid. She needed all the help he could invoke.

He remembered his initiation when he received his Bogo bag of stones at seven years old. At that age, their village culture deemed children old enough to participate in the life of the village. They ceremoniously received their family name for the first time and were allowed to select their moonstones. The elemental forces in the stones provided help for them, especially at times of the full moon. The village members celebrated their introduction to the use of energy.

He learned a lot about the energy of the moonstones from times when his body needed help after some misadventure, or for guidance in making a decision. He took his bag off of his belt and dumped it in front of him. While she rested, he took the time to do his stone ritual and check with his body in case it needed any help after the day's adventure. A brief meditation opened his awareness to his biofield and the elemental spirits weaving healing webs to restore balance after such an emotional day. He came out of his reverie to realize that he'd better eat something and bed down for the night.

After finishing a meager meal, he rinsed his dish and rolled out his bedroll, glad that he decided to bring it along. He must keep the fire stoked through the night to keep her warm. He lay against an old log and closed his eyes.

No matter how he tried, sleep avoided him. He needed time to process the changes in his life this girl created. When he studied her face, he knew she was the special one he had been waiting for. *Why did we have to meet here of all places? Why did I have to rescue her? It's so odd that she came to these same woods.* "Why?" he asked out loud. He understood that destiny always had a purpose and didn't create accidents even when events seemed so random. *Why are we here together?* he wondered. *Why have I been sent here? I know the stories about this place, but I still don't understand why we came at the same time.*

2. Remembering a Conversation with His Mother

As he lay there, he remembered one of his last conversations with his mother. At one point, he sat by her bedside when she woke up and said, "I've been given a message. The sun rose, and I was walking through some tall trees when an old woman appeared on the path in front of me. She greeted me by name and told me now was the time for the Sacred Heart to gather once again and for the Indwellers to return to their heartland." She often talked about her dreams. The family called her a Dreamwalker. From as far back as he could remember, the stories she told about her dreams held him spellbound. He missed those times.

Her dreams often concerned their ancient homeland, which she called Zathera. Tradition said it had been an ancient Panolarian mystery school. Many enlightened people believed Panolarians to be the first divine race of humans on earth. The school maintained a living memory of their origins, their history, and their destiny within the cosmic family. It thrived for over five thousand years, but as people slowly lost the memory of their connection to Source, the school closed. Some people stayed, but most felt they needed to go out into the broader population to interact with other cultures. In his travels, he found three other communities that still lived by the sacred path of harmony with the Earth.

"Who were the Indwellers?" he asked.

"My grandmother called them the founders of Panolaria, our heart and soul. They created Zathera by combining their life energies from Source. That force still holds the energetic balance for the whole planet," she said. "I feel that a re-emergence is about to take place. I don't know why, but the founding guardians need to come back together. Now I have a deeper understanding of some of my visions and dreams."

A strange look crossed her face, and she reached for his hand. "As I've told you before, Abe, I always knew you were a special child because you're a dreamer, too. Do you remember any of them?"

"Not really, although I have a faint memory of seeing a ball of light recently.

"That's right! A couple of times you floated around as if carried in a ball of light. I'm so glad you remember. Hold on to it and remember what it felt like inside your body. Hold on to that."

"I will."

"If you ever doubt who you are, remember that experience, that feeling. It can be a guiding force for you. If we remember those unusual childhood experiences, they can propel us forward in life. They are an internal witness from Spirit to remind us of our miraculous connection to Source. Without that conviction, life may become overwhelming, and you can slip deeper into density. Also, remember the cycles of life that I've taught you, Abe. For the first several years after birth, you live more in spirit than in your body. Your spiritual guidance is unhindered during those years when your body is growing rapidly and you're learning to use it. "From five to seven years of age, children begin to leave those early years behind. They forget about their imaginary friends and enter the early stages of mental development. During the next seven years, the remnant memories of their prenatal life disappear, and they start to develop an inner life, their own feelings, and a mind of their own. It becomes quite possible to develop self-centeredness at this stage unless understanding adults intervene to help them see that others have feelings, too. You are turned inside out, so to speak, and your spiritual connection fades away. With the onset of puberty, the rational forces develop as well to help the young person learn self-control and choose what's best for them. Above all, they need to come to an awareness of their sacred heart — their inner Source connection. I know you know all of this, but I want to remind you how important it is."

She continued, "I've seen it, Son, future generations of people who've lost their balance and moved totally to one extreme. They lose all awareness of their own, indwelling Source. Earth will fall into a great sleep. It already has, but it gets much worse. This deep sleep will only end when the pain inside becomes unbearable. An inner stirring will haunt them, a feeling that something is missing in their lives. This search will take them inside their bodies. Their bodies will begin talking, and they'll learn to listen."

***

An owl hooted in a nearby tree, bringing him out of his reverie. Another hoot followed, then another. It seemed like an old friend talking to him. The feeling arose to take a look at the world through the eyes of the owl to be able to see with clarity, no matter how dark. Unexpectedly, his day turned dark with trauma and struggle, but the two of them worked through it. A feeling of déjà vu swept aside the darkness. The two of them had walked together in these woods before. They shared great happiness. *Was this what Mother was trying to tell me?* he wondered.

***

His mother's words came back to mind. "After this age of darkness, people will re-discover their inner connection to the source of life that existed before the coming of the dark Lords. The mysteries will be unlocked. What we try to keep alive becomes the answer. What we etched into our physical codes will begin to stir. The great awakening thus begins because we dared to restructure our genetics to change the future. That is who we are. We shine the light for the future. We've resurrected a sleeping physical code that was turned off. This marks the return of life, love, and joy to the masses of humanity. We are the hope for humanity, Abe. Never forget that."

"I get it, Mother. I understand. I'll teach my children what you have taught me. I'll keep our sacred path alive."

"Good. I trust you. I just felt the need to explain this again. Abe, you are one of the original guardians. I understand this now. You must go back. It is time for the return; a gathering is being called. You will help repair our broken state. All of you will collectively repair the distortion in the grid that keeps our physical genetics in bondage. You will reverse what has been, and give life to a new paradigm that will lead mankind down a different path than what they know now. Otherwise, we may destroy ourselves as well as the planet. I've seen that possibility, but I decree it will not happen. You must go and rewrite everyone's destiny. You must go start a new life there. From the other side, I will be there to help you. My body won't let me stay. I am needed over there for a while. I've done what I needed to do, and now it's your time, so go do it."

He listened intently, taking it all in.

Son, I've said enough for now. Trust the path laid out before you. You came into this lifetime to do great work, so trust in your inner guidance the way I've taught you, and you'll do splendidly."

She held his hands for a few, quiet moments. Tears began to stream down her face. A deep sense of loss engulfed him, and tears welled up in his eyes. They held each other for some time.

"I am so proud of you. Don't you ever forget it!"

He lifted his head from her chest, took her face in his large hands, looked into her eyes, and said, "I could not have had a better mother than you. I'll be ok. I love you so much. It's going to be hard without you, but I know I can do it. Thank you. I love you." After another embrace, they held each other's hands.

"How do I find this place?" he asked.

"Follow the setting sun until you get to what is now called the Caldarin Mountain, or Forest as some people say. It will take a few days to get there. You've heard it called the haunted forest. You've heard all the stories about it. You will no doubt hear many more stories along the way that may give you some guidance as well. I recommend not telling anyone that you are going there. I think you will have no problem finding it."

"The legend says that the path to Zathera leads past a bluff on the mountain with a beautiful waterfall. The entry is thick with stones and boulders that make it difficult to enter. It's believed to have once been a sacred and powerful stone circle. It is the energetic doorway to Zathera. The waterfall and the remaining standing stones are a Zatherian signpost that welcomes the self-aware traveler. It is assumed that if an unenlightened person tries to enter, the mountain will turn on them because they don't hold the legacy of awareness."

"Furthermore, rings of light guard the door to Zathera. These rings support a dome that surrounds the whole sacred mountain range. My mother called it the Center of All Life. It holds the whole planet in balance. When mankind started forgetting their connection to the Mother, Zathera and one other portal were created to preserve a remnant for the future."

"What happens to someone who goes there unprepared?" he asked. "I've heard a lot of scary stories about the forest, but why does it have to be a fearful place? This is something I have never understood."

"To establish a village like this as well as a Mystery School there, the environment had to be protected with this field," she replied. "The people there who still embodied that ancient awareness needed protection from outsiders who had no respect for that land. The beauty of the place tends to draw people to it even though they aren't compatible. If someone enters this hallowed ground unknowingly, they will be tested. The dissonance will generate consequences for them. They will be chased out by their inner demons because of the discord between their life and the life of the Earth. If they are a fear-generator, their lifestyle will block them from getting very far. The old native principles still exist on that mountain. No one can stay without them. Darkness can't stand the light that's reflected in that place, so it will flee."

"I'm glad that we can have this conversation," she added. "I never forgot the images that the old stories created in me. They'll help make it easier for you," as she patted his hand. "Now, you will be able to find the old ruins," she said.

Aside from the old stories, this was the first he'd heard about the proper way to enter Zathera. Thoughts of this adventure excited him, even though he had some guilty feelings, but he recognized them and chose to let them go. "Thank you, Mother, I look forward to it," he said with a warm smile.

"Good, good, that is the way it should be." She patted his hand. "Now, I am giving you my source mantle, which I received from our ancestors, and you will one day pass it on to one of your choosing. As you integrate this, your heart-mind becomes infused with all of the wisdom and understanding held in our family's Life Tree. We go back to the very beginning of the Aut'ma'hon race. We're one of a few remaining bloodlines that still carry the original omnipresent template. Our race goes back to before the time the extra-terrestrial invaders spliced their physical genetics into those first hominid races. We were able to throw off a certain amount of genetic contamination by staying true to our spiritual lineage. This is the only way to override what they did, revise it, and still maintain our original connection with our omnipresent Source. Our Source knows itself. We are of one shared heart, and you now carry all that I am and all that has ever been, as well as all that ever will be in the future. Because you live, we all live through you. Abe. Know I am always with you, especially through what I have just given you."

He began spinning from the tremendous download flooding through him, all the while transfixed by his mother's beautiful eyes, as she transferred all of the ancient wisdom she held, all of the knowledge and reminiscent memory that her family tree had ever experienced.

"Go, go. Do what you must, and let me rest for a while."

***

The hoot owl spoke to him again, like an old friend who stopped by with a few friendly words of encouragement. His thoughts returned to home, this time to his uncle. Part of his preparations in getting ready to leave included transferring everything over to his uncle because Abe knew he would never be back. His uncle agreed to take care of his mother until she made her transition. He assured Abrum that he would complete all of her death rites of passage, as he did for all members of their village. His friends called him the death angel. His calm and joyful spirit helped troubled souls to make their transition. If need be, he would stay with a person for weeks until they finally released their body. Even after they passed, he would continue to guide them through the many layers the body had to shed before their soul could enter the dead zone.

After Abe's father passed while Abe was quite young, his uncle became the only father he knew. He took Abe and his young cousin on overnight excursions and taught them how to hunt and fish. One night a bear wandered into their camp. His uncle stood guard over them with a burning stick from the campfire until the bear satisfied his curiosity and left. That made a lasting impression on his young mind. He learned admiration and respect for the animal.

After he gained some maturity, his uncle allowed Abe to accompany him when he cared for a dying villager. Abe learned more each time. Some people were very alert and peaceful and enjoyed the companionship of friends and family to the end. Others struggled for a long time. With those people, his uncle would often play his lyre to help them relax and let go.

"Pay attention to the body," he told Abe. "It will always tell you what it needs. In some cases, such as an accident, they may not be prepared to separate from the body and will get stuck in the trauma. You can talk to them. They will listen to you and follow your instructions. This also releases the loved ones they leave behind."

"So many people fear exploring the subject of death," he continued. "To live life, you must understand that the physical body has a right to live. It needs to be honored and respected so it can gain self-awareness during its lifetime. The physical body can learn at any age, just as the mental body can. Our body was created to help us discover who we are."

By observing the death process, Abe learned the difference between someone who had developed a full-body consciousness and those who ignored their bodies. A struggle developed when it came time to disengage from the physical structure that was only a convenience, simply a tool to meet the needs of the moment. Such spirits often became stuck as they tried to withdraw and ended up chained to the corpse. Family members would pick up on this and continue their mourning at the grave site for extended periods.

On the other hand, someone who found joy in living, grateful for the body that made it all possible, disengaged from it easily. They realized that a new experience awaited them on the other side, just as it did each morning after going to sleep the night before. The goal of incarnation was to gain the experience of self-awareness through life in the body and the joy of choosing to love life and other living beings.

Young people learned to understand death by preparing their death cosmology and using it as a guide throughout their lives. This cosmology represented a blueprint for the creation of an ideal embodiment during their next life and the strength of the soul to fulfill that plan. The right to choose the best possible life belongs to all omnipresent beings and affirms their ownership of their destiny. This blueprint continuously changed as they grew in knowledge and wisdom and gained access to their inner guidance. By maintaining this practice, they wouldn't default to other people making decisions for them. Instead, they learned to feel what was appropriate for them as contributing members of human society rather than self-centered consumers.

His uncle taught him all this. The memory brought home to him how much he would miss him in this new life. He became a major part of his childhood after his father passed. Abe learned a lot, and now he needed to pass it on. His mother taught him much about life, while his uncle mentored him in the art of dying and its rites of passage. As he thought about this, he realized he wished he'd taken the time to just sit and talk with his uncle before he left. It might have been the last time he would see him. That thought saddened him. He resolved to visit him at some point. With all his preparations, it hadn't dawned on Abe how much he would miss his uncle.

***

After all his affairs were in order, Abe stayed by his mother's side a little longer and read to her out of the Book of the Dead. She talked about what she envisioned for her next embodiment, and he finally achieved some closure concerning her imminent passing.

He remembered their final conversation.

"Are you ready to go?" she asked.

He nodded. They both wept as he held her head next to his. Finally, she pushed him away and took his face in her hands.

"Son, you are my heart. Remember that. We are One, and what you do I also do. I love you always."

"I know, Mother."

"I almost forgot. I want to give you some things that my mother passed on to me. I want you to take them and give them to one of your children. Go over to my box on the table."

Inside, he found an amber amulet and a small emerald like the ones his father had given him. He picked them up and took them over to her.

"Oh, I loved this piece," she said as she turned it over and looked at the familiar symbol etched on its back. "The sacred flame," she said out loud as she ran her finger over it one last time. "Do you remember what it means?"

"Yes, I do. It represents our quest to find our own heart's Pink Pearl."

"You remember the legend, right?"

"Yes."

"Good, good. Remember it and pass it on as we all do."

"I will, Mother."

"Abe, go over and see if there are any other keepsakes you might want."

He sorted through the items in the box, selected two, and thanked her for them. He gave her a reluctant kiss, and she told him to go to bed. "You have a long day ahead of you."

"Yes, you're right," he said sadly. "You sleep well."

"You, too, Son."

The next morning, his uncle and a few close friends came to say their goodbyes, and he hugged and kissed his beloved mother one last time. He walked out of the only home he had ever known, tears streaming down his face. The spirit of this place bonded to him deeply. It provided his strength. He thanked it for all it had given him. He silently bowed to it and to all of the elemental spirits that had been his playmates as a child. When he shifted his focus, he could see them even now. Some gathered to see him off. Two fairies popped up on his visual screen.

"We want to go with you."

"Really?"

"Yes. The whole clan chose us to travel with you. We also have a legacy in Zathera. Can we come along?"

"Well, of course," Abe told them. "I'm glad to have you both." His spirits lifted as his companions landed on his backpack.

A nearby cave came to mind where he spent a lot of time with them and his uncle. You could reach a spring deep inside. His uncle would often treat people there because of the powerful, beneficial mineral spirits in the water. It bubbled up some distance from the opening, so one had to carry a torch to reach it. His uncle dug out several earthen mud baths to use along with the spring water. Even a young person like himself could experience a sense of rejuvenation from a full-body immersion in the earthy minerals. "Thank you, old friends, I will miss you, too."

On impulse, he turned around to take one last look at his home and saw his uncle and friends standing on the porch. He waved and placed his hands over his heart, bowing respectfully to them. This gesture indicated the highest esteem for the other person, a salute from the cherished divine presence that lived within each soul. It was their normal form of greeting that made a connection from their sacred space without absorbing any noxious energy that may have been attached to the other person's field. This avoided any connection to the collective circuitry.

Telepathically, he told his uncle that he would send word when he arrived safely. It hit him again that he would never see his mother in this life. He accepted all those feelings of loss, now tempered with excitement for the adventure ahead of him. He picked up his energetic tail and sucked it within himself for safekeeping. He would extract it again when he got to his new location and anchor himself on the grid.

He took several deep breaths as he walked down the road that would lead him on his search for the Caldareon Mountain.

3. Traveling Back to Original Separation

Abe dealt with his own trauma when his father died suddenly. His young age meant that it took him a long time to get over it, but with his mother's wise guidance, he succeeded. Using this experience, he helped one of his friends face the same trauma. This case, however, sounded like it would take him into some very unusual territory based on his mother's remarks.

I'm not sure how to go about doing this, but she needs my help. He quietly sat down beside her so as not to disturb her. He closed his eyes, took several deep breaths, and set the intention to align his breathing with hers.

I need to remember Mother's mantle. I'm sure it holds everything I will need. He placed his hand on her chest so that he could feel her breath. Once his breathing matched her rhythm, he set his intention to synchronize their frequencies. *We are still strangers but we are in perfect harmony.* He sat quietly waiting until a curtain of consciousness opened over his present awareness: the woods, the owls, the moon, the two of them next to each other. He felt himself move across a bridge and into a presence, a musical awareness, a harmonious tone from two instruments, two hearts in one, divine consciousness. This would be their vehicle to go wherever they needed to go.

From this space, he called out to her: *Hello? Hello? I'm the one who came to your rescue today. I mean you no harm.* She made no immediate reply. He sensed a shroud of darkness around her. She probably had no more experience with this type of communication than he did, but he hoped that the light he directed toward her would help to wake her up to his presence.

Hi. I am Abe. I sensed you might need some help. Are you okay?"

I ... I think so, she said. Then she spoke slowly as she said *I am Tythea.*

Do you remember your accident?"

I'm beginning to.

I'm here to help you. I've been trained to work with trauma. After I reached you, you passed out because of the pain, and you're still unconscious.

Ok.

When you lose consciousness like this, you go into your pain body. A part of you still lies trapped there. Do you understand?

She hesitated. *I guess so.*

I know this seems strange, communicating outside of the body, but we can talk oversoul to oversoul. By working together from this level, I can help you heal some genetic trauma that contributed to your fall. First of all, you need to realize that your fall was not an accident. We planned it long ago so that we could access this pain layer that we're on, ok?

She was silent for some time. *If you say so. You've helped me remember falling into the pit, but I can't access my guidance. Can you help me with that? I feel scared and lost.*

He feared she might not stay with him. *Can I … can I scoot closer to help support you?"*

Yes, she said. *Help me if you can. I don't know what to do. I'm confused.*

That's what I'm here to do, he said. *Let's first set an intention to bring our breathing into sync. Then, I'm going to harmonize my frequency with yours, and we'll use your oversoul layer to get to the bottom of this, okay?*

Sure, I'm with you. I will shadow you. Wherever you go, I will go.

Breathe … just relax and let go. Allow yourself to find that part that's still trapped in fear and pain from the accident. As you go through this process, be aware that you stand as a proxy for your entire genetic tree, past, present, and future, as well as for all mankind. The two of us will stand in for everyone.

Next, we're going back, and you are going to allow yourself to energetically relive your experience. Be aware that the only way for you to diffuse an old trauma comes through unconditional love, divine love. It can neutralize any past triggers, like judgment. It bridges time and space. I'm sure you already know this kind of love. It can heal any unresolved issues. When this love becomes a part of you, you become the observer rather than the participant who's trapped in the emotion of the moment. You move into the unconditional moment, free to examine each moment on its creative merits alone. From this place, you are the writer, editor, and director of your life. Do you understand?

Yes, I'll make that my intent.

Ok. You're ready. Go back to that moment and feel the shock of falling into that hole, then pull yourself out of it, returning to this safe and protected place. Notice that every trigger you might feel is a gift, not a curse. Decree that.

He paused, watching her reaction. She seemed calm.

You could easily be triggered by a lot of stuff that we might run into as we do this, so you need to be prepared. Are you ready? The fog around her thinned a bit.

'Y, yes,' she stammered.

Remember, think of every trigger that comes up as a gift, a key to greater understanding. Simply observe it and hold the frequency of unconditional love. Don't go into it. Use it to transform the emotions. You are installing the ability to stay present and make the necessary decisions. I will remain with you. Divine guidance is always there to help you, representing your ability to know intuitively what to do, an ability taken from us long ago by the invaders who disconnected us from our Source. Remember?

Yes, yes, I know, she said.

Good, good. Are you ready?

She nodded.

My mother warned me that we are going back to our original cause. We will revisit the experience of our original separation from the Source and the subconscious imprint that we still carry. It's the combined Mother-Father God's original experience. We need to watch it so we can gain an understanding for ourselves of what happened, and repair our physically and spiritually damaged genetics. Remember, as you go through this introspection, you represent all of your ancestors. As you heal, you will also heal the past, present, and future generations.

He asked again, *Ready?* She nodded. *Is it okay if I put my arm around you?*

You need to feel my support?"

Yes, that's okay, she responded.

Let's breathe together, and then you take it from there.

Okay, she said. *I will relive my experience with full awareness. I can maintain my consciousness,* she declared.

I'm falling. I'm in the pit now. Oh, the pain is terrible. Remember you are not your pain, he reminded her.

Okay, what are my triggers? I can feel without going into the pain. I can feel a balance point. I am on my pain grid.

She followed the grid and shot through several hazy planes until she and Abe came to a screeching halt over the top of a darkened, murky-colored grid. They floated there for several moments while she breathed to maintain her observer mode in this strange place. She felt the pull of several strong ancestral collectives.

Abe whispered telepathically, *You are safe, no matter how strange this feels. Release any fears. Breathe and stay focused. Through the vehicle of unconditional love, you are out of time and space. From here, you can access the Earth records. Reinforce your sacred connection again. It is your protection. It keeps you out of any negative energies. Remember: they can't vibrate at this frequency.*

Her hologram shifted as she re-aligned her various bodies. She re-stated her centering mantra a few more times while visualizing herself immersed in pink light. *I rest in the presence of divine love.* With her alignment in place, she decreed her intention to access the origins of separation with the help of a grid tracker. In a flash, they left their present reality and sped through one-dimensional plane after another. They slowed down abruptly and found themselves up against a wall blocking them from going any farther.

Hold here for a moment, Abe said. *Let me tune into all of this to decide what to do. This is new for me. I have never traveled back this far, back before our reality even started,* he whispered. He shivered as several energetic alignments slipped into place. *The ancients are telling me what our next step needs to be. They're saying we both must maintain our pink vibration. This wall can't stop us because we're in a different, parallel plane. We see it, but they tell me it can't stop us. It's a barrier the invaders coded into our genetics, and for some reason, we needed to see it. Keep going. Ask to be taken where we need to go. Let's re-center again and get back into sync."*

The view rippled slightly as they started to move again. This time, they disappeared into the structure of the wall. He sensed they now hung in space between two grids.

We're here. That's what I'm hearing, he said.

Their consciousnesses began acting as one entity. From this observation point, they saw a spinning field out ahead of them. She led Abe as they approached the field and asked for the ability to understand it. Several deep breaths aligned her field with the energy in front of her. *I reaffirm that I'm an observer and I am neutral. We have come to understand what originally happened and what caused mankind to go down this path in the first place. What caused our downfall? Why did we lose our connection to Source? We've heard the stories, but we want to see for ourselves.* With their breathing still aligned, they both took several deep breaths. Something shifted in their bodies. Holding their unified consciousness, she called for their internal guidance to act as an interpreter for what they now experienced. As it emerged, they saw an ancient presence that slipped from humanity's collective memory long ago. Its energy penetrated every fiber of their being like sunshine on a warm beach, flooding their awareness with the consciousness of its being and the secrets of the universe within it. They became one living essence.

I am your omnipresent self, a voice said. *I am here to guide, protect, and communicate with you while you're in this zone. Realign your vibration to my frequency before we proceed.*

They took several deep breaths to merge their energy with it. Consciousness faded into nothingness, except for a slight awareness of nothingness. A strong shudder shook Tythea from head to toe as a new energy moved into her. Their guide gradually increased their sensitivity until they felt light moving out of them into the distance. They synchronized themselves again to maintain one mind with this new perception.

Yes, be of one mind.

Both of them relaxed as this light pierced one genetic barrier after another, releasing any inherited chains as it did so. They entered a state of bliss, aware of so much ancestral garbage. The power of this out-of-body experience forged an unbreakable bond in the moment.

Now what? she said.

We need to set up our intention before going any further, Abe responded. *Close your eyes. What are you sensing?*

A new place, another time. I have never traveled through time in an altered state like this before, let alone gone this far back. I'm so happy that you are here to guide me through this. What exactly am I supposed to do? Okay, yes. I am the doorway that they must go through. I'm connecting into the female side of my genetics. A man would go through the male side. I'm to access my mother's ancestral lineage.

Abe sensed her confidence returning. *That's what we were taught; be aware of the frequency of the dimension we're in and attune to it.*

I need to find out what happened in the original cause. What happened in the beginning? How did it imprint on the whole history of mankind? I hear something. I hear that we are a reflection of that event that sent us down this evolutionary path. It is what's keeping humanity rutting in this old programming of misery and pain. War after war echoes across the land. Life isn't lived in peace and joy. A frown crossed her lips. *What did happen?*

She took another deep breath. They had drifted into a new plane, but he couldn't get a read on it at all. Off in the distance, two distinct energy fields overlapped slightly in the middle. They had gone as far back as they could go, to the beginning of their re-organization as a species. These two represented the two parental aspects at the beginning of creation.

From their teachings, they understood that extra-terrestrial visitors came to this planet and started experimenting on the hominid species. As a culture thousands of years more advanced than the hominid species on Earth at the time, they knew how to genetically alter the hominid's chromosomes. Repeated modifications gradually created a much different species. Eventually, the chromosomes split into two, creating separate males and females. Before this, all individuals were androgynous. This split created an energetic gap when the extraterrestrials ripped apart these two primary aspects of human creation. This experience of being torn in two became the root of so many of mankind's problems. This separation is the fall that sent the species into a spiraling descent away from inner Source.

Abe and Tythea slowly approached the closest field. *Realign,* he reminded her. They picked up an energy that felt lonely and scared, the Mother. *I'm tuning into the Mother,"* she silently said to Abe. *She feels cold. There's a cold aching in her bones. I don't know if I'm properly interpreting what she feels.* She returned to her observations. *I can hear the Mother's thoughts. She doesn't remember being warm, but I believe I can find that experience.* She sent out a signal in search of this warmth.

They followed the force of the Mother's will into the darkness toward the second energy field. This one felt much different; apparently, the Mother's counterpart, the Father. He also seemed lost and afraid and, even more confused and angry. He appeared to be blind and helpless.

I feel like we should help, Tythea said to Abe.

We must maintain our neutral zone, Abe reminded her.

They watched both the Mother and the Father reaching toward each other, unable to bridge the gap. Abe understood that neither realized they were already in each other's fields. *They feel confused and deeply disturbed,* Tythea said.

A huge, flaming, red ball of energy emerged from the Father field. Abe and Ty stared, transfixed at the show playing itself out in front of them. The Father figure bent backward. Suddenly, the flaming ball leaped from him. He opened his mouth as if screaming at something in the darkness, but no sound came out. The Father momentarily straightened up and then collapsed in sheer exhaustion.

Ty recoiled from the shock of what they witnessed. Abe could tell that all of her energy had drained from her field. Father God acted completely unaware of what he created. Abe and Ty watched as the ball of energy slowly uncoiled until it was free of its embryonic confines. For a moment, it hovered there. *It looks like it's searching for a target,* Abe whispered.

Suddenly, the cloud of energy flew off across the crusted surface of the grid in the direction of the Mother. Ty opened her mouth to scream out a warning to the Mother, but hesitated. *Careful,* Abe cautioned. *You've lost your neutral observer mode,* he said. *You aligned with the Mother. Focus on your breath again to realign and move back to your center. Maintain your neutrality.*

Ty turned to the Mother. *What are you experiencing now?* she asked. The Mother remained calmly floating. *I don't think she is aware of what just occurred,* said Ty. She turned to Abe. *Can you feel that? She's giving off a feeling of deep longing, wanting to be reunited with her dream lover.*

Abe remained silent, watching the scene in front of them.

I did sense something. I know I did. Ty said. *I'm picking up on the Mother's thoughts. She senses that something is approaching her in the darkness.*

Ty and Abe waited with the Mother in anticipation. They watched as the energy reached her. They could feel her thoughts: *Why do I think that it is male, that he is my lover?* the Mother thought. *Why am I feeling so jumbled up? He's coming, he's coming. That's all that matters.*

The Mother Goddess prepared herself for her visitor, but the two observers noticed a huge shift in her energy as the light came closer. *Something is wrong*, Ty said.

The Mother's pink, loving vibration changed. The vibration she picked up on pursued her, but the resonance felt wrong to Abe and Ty. The Goddess began to close her heart, and the pink turned to a deep red. *She senses danger approaching and is throwing up a protective shield around herself*, Ty whispered. Whatever approached the Mother showed no signs of love. The Mother found no place to go, no place to hide. She stood strong, ready to resist. The light stopped in front of her and stretched itself upward in a threatening posture. Ty and Abe flinched in the face of so much rage. It took the appearance of a snake with glowing red eyes staring at the Mother. It arched backward, seething with rage. It lunged at the Mother, then disappeared into the night.

The observers felt the Mother Goddess' inability to comprehend what had just taken place. Abe could tell that Ty struggled to regain her composure. *I feel as if that blow hit me.* Ty's energy flickered, then strengthened again.

The Mother stood there, her arms clenched around her once beautiful, etheric body. Abe and Ty sensed her surveying herself in slow motion. Pieces of herself floated around her body. Her upper diaphragm had a hole in it, and part of her heart was missing. Abe whispered, *She can't comprehend the trauma or pain, as if she never experienced anything like that before.*

Dramatic change swept through the Mother's etheric body. Her whole energy field changed from a golden light to a dark, dirty, reddish-brown around her wounds. An angry heat spread throughout her midsection. As it grew in intensity, the energy oozed out of her body, filling in the gaping hole. Instead of a true, regenerative healing energy that the Mother needed, the darkness created a kind of pseudo-repair. This energy appeared to bond itself to the other parts that had been torn away, now floating in space.

Her repair isn't working, Ty said.

It's not compatible with her energy, Abe replied.

The observers noted the pain distorting the Mother's once radiant beauty. She doubled over with a scream of agony. The scream ejected something from her mouth, which stretched itself into a dirty, yellow garment to cover her as she fell unconscious. The two read her last thought before the darkness released her from the pain: *Why?* The old form of the Mother disappeared under this new essence.

Ty wondered to Abe, *what did she just give birth to? Was this painful separation of Mother from Father the beginning of the emotional body and the birth of the pain body? Oh, my! We've just witnessed its emergence.*

This is what we are here to understand, responded Abe.

Abe, said Ty, *the attacker meant to kill the Mother, but instead, the pain body that she birthed is trying to heal her.*

This insight gave them a new perspective. The Father gave birth to rage and fear of the unknown, and the Mother birthed rejection and pain. They saw the pain body clinging to the Mother's lifeless form, distraught and full of deep fear. No one was there to help.

A voice said *Maybe it's not as bad as it looks. Play like you're not hurt. Rise above the pain so that you don't feel it.* This energy from the two of them spawned another separation that began to disassociate itself from the pain. Out of that layer, they saw several energies fly around the body, twisted in pain.

Escape and denial were born here, Abe whispered. The little imps gathered up the debris and disappeared with it into the wound, trying to magically heal the damaged areas. The twisted form relaxed as these new thoughts flew around, but Abe could see that none of this helped. The Mother didn't recognize dark energy for what it was, instead suppressing and stuffing it in some dark crevice to be forgotten. Because the Mother didn't understand it, this violation couldn't be transformed through unconditional love and acceptance. The Mother's near-lifeless form couldn't release judgments against the emotional body. Instead, the physical body was programmed through the attack to deny anything that felt threatening or painful.

Oh, that's why healing isn't complete, Ty said. *This layer stuffs the pain somewhere rather than feeling it. The dark energy isn't being changed at all. How many times have I done this? Wow, this is a wake-up call! I need to study this before I work on someone else.*

Up to this point, the Mother and her place in creation hadn't been understood. In her original state, she connected to the Source of All That Is, whole and complete in herself, a sovereign intelligence within the body.

What Abe and Ty witnessed revealed a piece of history that the elders taught them while growing up. They saw both Mother and Father, isolated and confused, and an androgynous union split in two, left to their individual misery. *So, this is what the elders were talking about,* Ty said. *This upsets me because I don't understand what we just witnessed.*

Abe responded, *Breathe. Refocus on your center. Stay in unconditional love. Remember, no judgments. Forgive them because we know what they are doing. I remember my mother telling me about this event. She said,* "To this day, everyone carries the energy of this split buried so deeply in their body that they can't retrieve it."

We came to change that," Ty said. *"We are the hope for humanity. Okay, I understand this now. I invoke the right for all mankind to stay present amid trauma, to maintain our seat on our throne, and to make our own decisions as individuals. We can choose to stay present. We can maintain our connection and receive guidance during a traumatic event. We can believe there is more to life than pain and suffering. We must change our programming. Knowing our origins and our connection to Source, we can heal this. I bring this online. This has got to change.*

Oh, my gosh, Ty said to her astral companion, *some of those little imps we saw earlier are the Mother's new offspring, the egos that took over when she lost consciousness. After she fled, someone had to run the body and keep it alive while she gave up control, which is exactly what we do when we are too scared to handle a situation. I see it so clearly now.*

Yes, Abe observed as she paused, apparently in deep thought.

Doing this repeatedly creates a pattern that allows our egos to take over, Ty continued. *I've seen myself do it, our whole society does it. We're programmed to duck and run for cover if our life gets too intense, so someone has to take charge to keep the body going.*

Abe continued her thought. *An ego is born out of our psyche to take care of the problem, but then becomes a permanent member of our unconscious family because we don't change our behavior.*

Yes, replied Ty. *I finally get it. When I understand that I can deal with whatever life brings me, I will gain control of my fear, choose the right course of action, and dismiss the egos that continually hang out on my doorstep. Good choices are birthed out of intuition, which is the product of confidence, determination, and above all, unconditional love for who we are. Pain is a teacher, not an enemy. I forgive myself,* she said, *"because I didn't understand it before seeing this. We can heal ourselves. Inspiration and intuition can give us feedback as we process our experiences.*

You must choose to stay present in every moment of your life, Abe said. *Decree this intent. Love is the key. Accept what happened because it has brought you to this moment. You must consciously work to repair this in your genetics, heal your present life, and change your future. The future for all of humanity.*

The storm they witnessed passed. This new understanding broke through like the noonday sun, warming them through and through in a gentle, loving embrace. Abe watched it move through her and spread out in all directions to touch everyone willing to receive it.

I feel something pulling on me, like floating downward towards me, Ty said. *I am reuniting with my body.* She opened her eyes. It came back to her that she had been hurt, he had rescued her, and they had been on this out-of-body experience together. *Oh, my, that was wild,* Ty said, still speaking intuitively.
"It was, wasn't it?" he said aloud.

***

"I have never experienced anything like it," she said, looking up into his face, into his eyes, really seeing him for the first time. "I am changed. I now see you like I couldn't before." She tilted her head slightly. "I see now such a tenderness about you. I couldn't see that before." Looking directly into his eyes, she reached a sense of understanding. "You felt it, too, right, everything that I did?"

"Oh, yes," he replied.

She wanted to search deeper into his eyes, to see his very soul. His compassion and unconditional love almost overwhelmed her. She had never felt this kind of gentleness before, especially with it directed towards her. She hesitated to move just to prolong the moment. He released his hold around her shoulders. A shudder passed through her soul, and she knew their intuitive linkup was now severed.

She hadn't experienced this connection with any other man except her father and a few other elders back home. She understood the importance of this experience. She knew that because of him, she could go so deeply into the mother's depth of despair. He supported and honored her unconditionally. She knew that with him, they could stand as a reflection of a couple who healed this original separation and restored the divine marriage. They both needed to mirror this from within for it to work. They both had to be here to heal from both sides. She becomes the bridge to reach other women ready to heal and bring their inner life into balance. She closed her eyes to observe the rips and tears in her own genetics and imagined a beautiful pink mist filling in the gaps, condensing into a delicate, sheer fabric, which attached to the sides of the gap, healing, bridging the great divide between Mother and Father.

She took several breaths to assimilate the pink essence bonding to her field. She watched the fabric solidify. *"The most ancient of all curses is being lifted!"* sounded deep within her mind. *"Not only a curse but a plague*!" Women would once again receive honor and respect as an equal part of creation.

4. Their Divine Astral Meeting

"That trip may have taken only a minute for all I know," Ty said, still within her astral awareness, *"but I feel as if our whole world changed into something new. My recent accident and injury now seem like a lifetime ago."* She rubbed the cut on her head. *"I feel a sense of well-being like nothing I've ever known before."*

Ty stared into Abe's eyes. *"This feels so natural, us being together,"* she said as Abe hugged her back. *"It feels like returning home after being gone for a long time."*

Abe stroked her hair. He knew that she now fully accepted him at every level. He experienced a strong sense of well-being. She began to cry.

"What's wrong, Ty?"

She looked back up into his face and blue eyes and kissed him.

She caught Abe completely off guard, but he willingly allowed her sweet, gentle kiss. He immediately felt his body respond in a way he had never felt before. *I've never kissed a woman before. Be quiet and just enjoy it,* he told himself. He let himself get lost in the sensation and responded with tiny little kisses all over her face. No one ever touched him in the depths of his soul like this. The moment became about recognition. *No, at this moment, it's not about sex. I'm not going there right now. I'm not going to disrespect her here. Sure, I'm attracted to her, but not now.* He felt the core of her soul. She held nothing back. She opened up completely to him. This kiss reconnected them. He felt it and returned the favor.

He surrendered to her kiss and the intensity of their newfound union, but an inner voice awakened that insisted on being heard. He tried to stay present to the feeling from Ty. *This is more complicated than you know,* said the voice. *Your heart has been filled with the recognition of someone dear to you, and you express that as only humans can. On the other hand, your body is programmed with strong hormones to reproduce as a being, reinforced by generations of behavior stored in your genetics. There is, however, a third option. You can be loving without being sexual.* To his body, this seemed completely foreign. *You can kiss without the need for anything more,* said the voice. Could he rewrite the ancient program in his hormones that insisted on procreation at the first opportunity? Could he restrain those deep, hidden forces until the two of them together could make a conscious choice to have a child? Could he be content to limit the expression of his affection to kissing? *Women were not made just to procreate, and neither were men. We're made to love one another as well as to have children.* When he understood that lesson, he set his intent to change his old programming to bring it in line with his new understanding. *May the divine Mother install this in our human template.*

When they slowly withdrew, he wanted to tell her what he experienced. *"Our kisses were a new experience for me. They stirred up something in my body and my soul. This seems weird, but when my body responded as a man, my soul said respond as a loving human being. Create something new for the male species. Kissing and having sex have always gone together, which often brings up the fear of being responsible for a child. It is clear as day now! Sex has become fearful because of this possibility. I've just installed a change in my old genetic programming. Until now, my body felt like some unknown force controlled it."*

Ty listened quietly. *"Yes, we started something here, but it's not finished yet."*

Referring to the experience they had with Mother and Father God, Ty said, *"I know that the trauma we saw gave birth to the emotional body."*

"I don't understand," Abe responded. *"What do you mean? I saw what happened. That's for sure. I saw a lot of pain."*

"It's hard to imagine that it never existed before this," she said with a slight frown on her face. *"I'm sure they felt pain but nothing like her first experience here."* Ty paused. *"We must find a way to heal this original imprinting of the collective pain body. The memory of this subconscious programming has kept everyone locked into suffering. If healing is to occur, this memory stored deep in the body must be understood so that it can be transformed. This is the root of our diseases, they stem from this primeval emotional damage. Our body remembers every detail of how it suffered when it went through this experience that separated us from Source."*

Abe understood the importance of her words.

Ty continued. *"If someone had addressed the issue, humanity could have found forgiveness and moved on, but we haven't. The body knows nothing has changed yet. We need to understand that the Mother is about movement. She can't be told to be quiet and pretend nothing happened when the emotional body is aroused."*

"If we can't change this for humanity," Abe said, *"the body will find a way to trigger those emotions again and again until they are resolved in a way that is not for our highest good."*

"Oh, and I must confess," she said, looking at him, *"I had to confront my fear when I felt the desire to kiss you. The voice in my head told me that I didn't even know you, but my heart said*

we've always known each other, so I pushed myself way past my comfort zone. I knew I needed to thank you with a kiss," she said shyly.

"Well, truthfully, I was kind of shocked, but I'm really glad you did. It brought a lot up for me, too. I think we needed to archive this understanding here on this energy band, the outer ring for Zathera. Anyway, that's what it seems like to me," he told her.

Without hesitation, she turned her body slowly around and leaned up against his chest.

"Are you okay with this?" she asked.

"Oh, sure," he said in her ear as he slightly nibbled it with a kiss.

"Good. I feel I'm done with my part here, so I'm turning it over to you so you can do your part." She sat silently, opening the space for him to do or say what he wanted.

"This is all new to me. My Mother tried to explain some of this, but I never really had any reference until now. I'm glad I'm here with you and that you can help me to understand it. Thanks."

"Thank you," she said, surprise showing in the tone of her voice. *"I'm glad you're here with me, supporting me. It's a miracle!"*

"I have a question about the Father," Abe said. *"Why was he so upset? I know we didn't go back that far to see why."*

"I wondered that, also," Ty responded. *"I can tune in, but I think you need to ask. You're the one who needs to understand this more than I do. That's what I feel, anyway."*

"Oh, okay. I need to set up my intent, don't I?"

He turned his consciousness inward to take a second, intuitive look at the moment of separation. This time, she would be assisting him. He knew she gave him valuable insight because he represented the males on the Father's side. He wanted to know why dark energy would come out of God. Isn't God supposed to be light? What caused the darkness? Another thing puzzled him. Why had the Mother seen the Father as light when he tried to kill her? Were there different shades of light? What happened to the Father to create this kind of energy? Why so much anger and rage? He couldn't imagine why Father God would do such a thing. He wanted answers to all of these questions. These questions deeply troubled him. He searched for some sort of foundation to get a toe-hold to start his search.

He forced himself out of his deep perplexity. He needed to be the bridge to the Father's side, a proxy for everyone to gain an understanding of the Father's experience when he realized he was all alone. He would have to be present and conscious because the Father seemed to be clueless about what happened. If he could view that event as a neutral observer, he might get some insight into the Father's behavior as well as clear up some major issues that the male gender has been carrying ever since.

Okay, what challenges males most? What about relationships with women? What Abe experienced earlier around sex had been his first trigger, so it seemed like a good place to start. Many men disrespected and belittled their wives and treated them as inferior. That always felt unsettling to him. A lot of men saw them only as sexual objects for them to use as they saw fit. Too many men felt no love for their wives at all.

The second issue for many men centered on their abuse of power. Once they reached a certain status, they lost all respect for those under them. A third issue involved the belief that to be strong, you had to be hardhearted because if you showed any feelings, you would be judged as weak. Bullying became all too common, also. He didn't like the way any of this felt.

Okay, this is enough, he told himself. *I've identified enough of these unloving vibrations. These examples should be enough to make my declaration. They'll stand as proxies for what we, as the male collective, need to change. I declare that all of us can learn from our mistakes, provided we're honest enough to face them. No one is perfect, and no one will ever know everything. I choose to learn and grow from everything I see and do. We have the power to heal the original distortion that damaged the collective hologram so long ago. This will set things into motion so that mankind can begin to heal the negative imbalance that has crippled every generation since then. Mankind will now be able to receive the help they have been praying for.*

With the two of them being able to travel back in time, they could replace the ignorance of the past with what they knew now. He again thanked his mother for teaching him that he possessed the power to change his genetics, past, present, and future. Here lay an opportunity for him to do just that. He had the right and the ability to repair the damage to the original grid that he inherited and restore it to balance. He wondered if the invaders behind the original separation knew what they had done in this respect. They probably did since they wanted to control humanity. Originally, humans existed in a freewill zone, but separation changed all that. Now fear controlled the lives of most people.

I forgive them, he quickly added when he felt his thoughts starting to rut in the destruction caused by the extraterrestrials. In this present moment, he and Ty hold the ability to repair the grid and offer humanity the capacity to heal.

The task before the two of them seemed overwhelming to him, but he took several deep breaths to calm himself down and set his intention once more. He mentally ticked off the topics he intended to cover in full consciousness. Now he felt ready to proceed.

He approached the grid around the Father and reminded himself to remain unconditional while he tuned in to the Father's frequency. *Maintain your center*, he repeated over and over as he projected himself back to the point of separation to take another look at the Father's energy. He immediately noticed a sense of utter confusion. *It feels like the Mother is getting it, too.* The feeling of being lost and afraid hit him. *Wow, he's feeling what the Mother experienced. He feels all alone and doesn't know what happened to him. He seems groggy, as if suddenly awakened, and is trying to figure out where he is. He's confused and doesn't remember anything. "* Abe could see the Father struggling to piece together little fragments of impressions in his mind, which frustrated him. It shocked Abe to realize that Father God could be ignorant about some things. He witnessed the birth of Father God, at least on this plane. Energetically, he was only a baby here. *I release any previous beliefs that contradict what I am learning,* he told himself. He began to understand the knowledge he received from his Zatherian family, that God was the Source within his soul, not an external ruler that other tribes worshiped.

As he watched, the Father's energy grew more agitated. The Father had been asleep and wanted to go back to sleep to escape the turmoil around him. But this unfamiliar state of affairs stopped him from slipping back into the comfortable darkness he had known. What woke him up? Abe scanned the scene surrounding him.

***

The Father God spent what seemed like hours trying to figure out the scene around him. He glared out into the darkness, searching for some slight glimmer of hope. His thoughts would stray as brief visions appeared, then quickly disappeared. He felt something out there. *Or was it in me?* he thought. Something pulled on him from out there. He tried to go after it, but realized he couldn't go very far for fear of the unknown. *I'm too afraid of the dark.* He wanted to go, but he couldn't find a way to leave this place. *Why can't I move? Why am I so afraid?* Finally, he forced himself to let it go.

A new awareness dawned on him: loneliness and the need to find someone. *What is lonely?* He was perplexed, curious, and angry. *All of these feelings seem to be bubbling up from somewhere deep below. I don't know how to deal with all this. Go back to sleep,* he ordered himself repeatedly. *Go to sleep,* he began to sing to himself. *This isn't working!* he blurted out in rage. *Go away*! he screamed into the darkness. He wanted answers, but at the same time, he wanted to punch someone or something. This emotion startled him because he didn't understand it. *I've gone mad, I'm all alone, and I'm angry about it.*

As his struggle continued, a quieter side emerged that gave him the impression that there was no one out there to blame. This felt good, and he entertained it for a while, but the other voice reasserted itself that someone was to blame. He felt two competing energies tugging on him.

He placed his arms over his chest as if remembering how it felt to hold someone. Or was it something inside? It rang true. His knowing pulled him inward as a bubbling memory made its way to the surface. As an understanding of this feeling grew in him, he felt a sudden jolt, like he had been slapped across the face. It snapped him out of his trance. Rage seethed inside him once the shock was over.

***

Abe trembled because he felt the shock. *Re-shift and re-balance*, he told himself. *Let it move right on through you. Notice the triggers, accept them, and move on — no judgments.*"

Remember, it's his. It's not yours, she whispered. *You're just observing.*"

Yes, yes. He took several deep breaths to quiet all levels of his body. He began to feel better and started processing his own experience.

He understood that the Father sensed that he needed the Mother. Some old feelings had come up, but this foreign aspect didn't want the Father to remember it. Before waking up, the two of them had been united as one. It didn't matter who moved;

separation created the disturbance. That's the source of all this confusion, but the Father didn't yet know that.

Abe's intuition helped him understand the Father's confusion. The Mother moved. She must have sensed something lost, broken. She searched for the problem.

Abe realized that neither of them liked where they found themselves. He didn't feel that they directed their frustration at each other. A third party created their distress. This invading energy carried an unloving darkness with it, blocking the Father from remembering their past union, keeping him restless, agitated, and angry. Abe felt this same lack of compassion. He needed to make this journey to fix what had broken.

The Father struggled with fear and rage. A dark energy pattern embedded itself in the Father's field. Abe could see two distinctive levels in his field that partially overlapped. The inner had a beautiful pinkish-white light in its core. But an expanding, deepening darkness overshadowed the light of the outer layer, chipping holes in the grid.

Abe felt the Father's confusion. The Father didn't know what to do with the feelings assailing him. He sensed that the Father felt another presence. He sent thoughts into the unknown. He waited and waited, but there was no reply, no sign of someone else. Abe felt the Father sinking into depression and despair. He watched the Father God wither up inside, searching for a way to escape his feelings, searching for escape in sleep that eluded him. Waves of desperation gave way to a desire for death. Abe could tell the Father neared a breaking point. He wished for death. He reached the breaking point.

Abe watched in startled disbelief as the Father suddenly arched his back and spewed a mass of dark energy out of his mouth, birthing rage, anger, and fear. In this fantasy state, he seemed ready to kill the source of his problem. He wanted revenge. This dark energy stoked his primal fire.

The Father didn't realize the power of this rage eruption. Now that it had been released, it immediately set to work to carry out the Father's wish, which was to attack the Mother. In this uncontrolled state, anger took over the Father. He blamed what he could not see, the Mother, for his pain and rage.

The extraterrestrial visitors had torn apart the two parental principles of Mother and Father, like separating the white of the egg from the yoke. The action left both of them stripped of their memory and blocked them from communicating with each other. Hidden behind this genetic manipulation lurked an alien agenda. They were a highly evolved race of genetic engineers who needed some new material for their dying bloodline.

Like a lightning bolt, Abe could see it: this newly born force manipulated its procreation to steal the Father's light and claim it for his own before anything else could emerge. It used fear and rage to hijack the ET agenda.

Yep, Abe realized, *a Luciferian program was hidden within their genetic changes to take control of creation after the split. Yes, I can see it all now, clear as a bell.*

After the genetic split, this first-born substance continued to use fear, anger, and every other emotional tool at its disposal to undermine the relationship between the two. It would weasel itself into the subconscious to promote discord of all kinds rather than harmony, war rather than peace. It wanted to take charge of the emerging human mind, to gain control of it before humans could learn to think for themselves and make their own choices. Abe remembered struggling with negative thoughts in his teenage years, thankful for his mother's and his uncle's guidance.

Now Abe understood what the invaders had encoded into the human genetics. What was once an androgynous, whole entity shattered, leaving two pieces needing to find a way to put themselves back together again. Here, at last, he understood the answer to the question: how could God do such a thing? God hadn't done it. The extra-terrestrial genetics broke humanity with this split. It took control of human behavior. Its created polarity. This realization hit him square in the face. *Wow! I can't believe I wasn't able to comprehend this before.*

As he pondered all of this, it dawned on him that this contrary energy made sure that it attached itself to the father's side, not the mother's. *Why choose the male side? Why create an egoistic energy? Why exclude her and set the stage for so much cruelty later on?* The realization hit Abe. *The Mother was the older, wiser aspect, the more mature, the womb of life.* Abe tried to make sense of the interaction between the two. The female side of the androgynous union reflected her life spirit as a supporter and protector. She evolved into a vehicle of motion. Movement operated as pure feeling through her physical form.

Originally, the male side was more of an overshadowing presence, an invisible force adding to her creational spirit. He shone his light on anything she did and followed her intuition and supported her decisions. Now he could see how he'd become more externalized and more detached, wanting to control everything she tried to do.

"Okay, I get it," Abe said. "His vulnerability, inexperience in physical matters, and the fact that he avoided internal awareness showed the invading energy that they could align with him, not the Mother."

The aliens separated the original being into male and female. Before, they worked as a unit, but now separation caused them to feel lost and afraid. They cut the internal and external aspects apart to insert their genetics, which stopped all previous communication that the two once shared. They saw the Father ripe for the picking. They could use him for their agenda. *I get it! I get it! I understand! In having him give birth first, they could infect her with their genetic material through the attack.* The severe injuries that she received mirrored the incision made by the invaders to alter the hominid's genes and bring them under control. The massive wound marked the spot.

The hominid also differed from other species on this planet in a remarkable way that they did not suspect. It was related to the universal Spirit, but their intervention disturbed this. They had no way to read the markers for spiritual genetics because they weren't a spiritual species. They were purely physical. They destroyed what had once been a harmonious relationship. He knew that was a harsh way to think about it, but from what he had observed, it seemed true. Of course, they didn't understand this, but this was the effect. The physical body's original ability to communicate with all parts of itself was disrupted. The invaders didn't have the universal perception to notice this unified field of intelligence. They were clueless in these matters. Consequently, the hominid went into a tailspin.

Abe took several deep breaths to assimilate all of this. It was a heavy load to bear. The realization that they destroyed the original omnipresent mind sent a wave of sadness through him. He forgave them for their lack of understanding even though a part of himself wanted to rage at them rather than forgive. *The universe allowed this to occur, so there must have been a strong reason. I must trust the Universe. Yes, they diverted our past, killed off an ancient race, and sent us on a journey we didn't choose, but we may understand it better as we gain more insights. We need to embrace the light of understanding and compassion. It's out of our hands.* With another processing breath, he released his need to be in control of everything.

He wondered why, with all of their abilities, the ETs did not have spiritual as well as physical genetics. If only they had evolved more spiritually, humanity wouldn't be in this conundrum. He couldn't change what happened, but perhaps he could bring some enlightenment to the misunderstanding around what's been called "light." Light doesn't necessarily mean it's automatically unselfish. Light comes in many degrees and shades. Just because you believe in spirit doesn't mean it's the light of love. There exists unloving light along with light that is love personified. One is universal, but one exists only in a purely physical dimension. The two have to be integrated to find balance. He understood that the light that the Father showed to the Mother didn't love itself. *That is the difference,* he told himself. *Don't forget it. You have to love who you are and not be so critical that you become fearful.*

Because the Mother had been a unified spirit all of her previous existence, she couldn't understand this new situation. She assumed that her lover sent the light, which meant he was approaching. That mistake caused her great confusion. She knew nothing outside of this realm. She couldn't comprehend this new reality. After this split, she felt isolated and cold. She wanted something, anything, to warm her up, so she opened herself up to receive the approaching light.

Okay, back to the light. I know I need to understand all of this in greater detail. Before the split, they existed as one being. Why would she respond by opening herself to any external energies? What did she imagine could possibly come to her from outside somewhere? He saw the connection to the warmth she sought, but why project it outward? *Oh, because of being separated, this new energy pulled her attention outward. When she saw the light, she sought it, wanted it, needed it. She opened herself freely to accept it.*

The male came into being as a result of separation. I am witnessing this as a male to stand as a proxy for my species. I've seen it, and now I understand it. I can choose to change my programming and archive it for others, as well.

He thought of his silent partner again. *Oh, yes,* he said, *I hear you. We are doing it together. Forgive me. We surrender the old mental body created by the ETs because we recognize the wrong done to the human race. We have the power through our connection to our inner source to change this. We choose to align with the light of unconditional love, not a foreign, unloving light that charges us with rage and fear. We chose to open a sacred space within our gestational womb to incubate these changes for the greater whole with the help of our divine source. We want to evolve, and grow, and remember that there once was an ancient, omnipresent mind, and we emerged from it. We align to this original intelligence,* he decreed for them. *That ancient mind can teach the younger mind how to surrender and work together.* He noticed that his silent partner was trying to get his attention. *Yes, what is it?* he asked gently.

***

I want to let you know that I agree wholeheartedly with your insights and affirmations. I know you included me, but I need to affirm my intentions for my proxy representing all women, as well. We, as a unified whole, need to declare this together. Also, we need to vow to unconditionally love and respect each other as equals, she added.

You're right. I think we need to do a little ceremony here to complete our transaction while we're still on this astral plane. I feel I have finished what I came here to understand. Do you agree?

She closed her eyes to see how his words felt. *Have I done what I needed to do?* she asked her omni-mind. *Is my part complete on all levels and in all bodies? Have I retrieved all the data that I need to take back with me to heal and repair the mother's genetics, or the lack thereof?*

She could see several last, energetic pieces slip into place in their combined field. For the first time, she intuitively saw two conjoined heart fields. It dazzled her. Earlier, she had seen dark threads weaving in and out of the outer layers of her heart, but now the darkness dissipated. It began to glow, and as she watched, their two fields grew brighter and brighter. She sent her intention into her body to perceive how everything was feeling there, as well. Her body felt like it had returned home after being gone for a long time.

Now, she had a road map of the trip they experienced, and everyone could use it if they wanted to. The grid supporting her physical body felt unusually light, bubbly, and blissful. All of the dark shadows of fear disappeared from her radiant heart field. Her genetics worked to free her from the ancestral programming. This free-flowing stream of love and joy spreading through her felt delightful, allowing it to be at home. The immune system no longer perceived joy and unconditional love as foreign invaders that should be exterminated. Now, they could become healing forces in the body to restore and lead it back to a state of balanced perfection. She turned her attention to her companion to tell him she agreed that they finished what they needed to do.

***

Abe explained a vision that showed him how to start their completion ceremony. They breathed in unison for several moments. He said, *I energetically call back all that was blown out of the mother's heart and diaphragm. To all of the pieces that floated away, I call you back to take your rightful place where you once were. I, Abe, stand as a proxy for all males. We came into materialization out of the split. As an awakening, conscious, omnipresent source, I declare that I have the right to call all of the mother's aspects back to her. I chose to stand as one aspect of her bridge. I forgive those who took us on the journey of separation. We have learned from this how to be and how not to be. I, as a male member of our species, chose to become whole and complete, and I assert my authority as the god of my being, a self-source-creator. To do this, I know that I must re-embrace the mother and bring her back within me. She is divine, and she is in me. I gladly accept this new divine light. I call all that was lost to come back in, and I consciously reverse engineer the old Adam and Eve imprinting of duality. I chose to release the light of rage that we unknowingly took in. I release the frequency of fear and replace it with the light of unconditional love as my guide from this day forth.*

He watched several dozen golden spheres of light out in the cosmos being magnetically drawn back together. Once all were in place, they floated towards them. He sensed Tythea watching with him. Their intensity strengthened as they drew closer until they exploded. Instinctively, they both jumped back and ducked as they watched a rain of golden, glittering sprinkles of light falling all around them. When the tiny lights reached them, each one exploded and disappeared into their energetic bodies. They opened their arms to receive this beautiful gift that symbolized the mother's heart and gut being repaired, and a part of them as well. Abe could feel the energy in his body and his biofield shift.

I'm feeling what true wholeness feels like.

All of his life he felt that he had to maintain a fake posture. He held himself together, spiritually, while waiting for his physical genetics to catch up with his perceptual changes. It felt a little artificial, but he had to give his body a chance to catch up. He was glad that was over.

I declare the lost have been found. They are now a part of my divine body.

He felt Tythea doing the same thing. Energetically, they held their arms open to receive what had been rejected so long ago. They were calling back their lost will essence that had been torn from the mother. They willed her return so that her divine essence could once again govern the body that she had created. It would take some time. Mature souls who embraced this new understanding would give their bodies the chance to reinstate what they originally knew. The heartfelt changes that they just set in motion would rewrite history and redirect future generations. They would reverse a lot of harm that the ETs did to human genetics.

***

Tythea whispered in her heart, *I welcome the return of my divine mother aspect, as well as the outer collective's. I welcome you, Mother; I return you to your rightful place in me.* Energetically, she felt teary-eyed. Unconditional love flooded her emotional body. *Divine Mother, I welcome your complete return in me. I also forgive those who didn't understand what they were doing to us back then. I know we gained more intelligence because of what they did, as well as other benefits, and I willingly release all the misery and pain that have been associated with it. I welcome your grace, your joy, and power in my life. I will live life with grace and ease because of your divine gifts. I will live my life with joy instead of hopelessness. I choose to be free.*

She quieted her thoughts, shifting her focus to check her heart's barometer. A light pink ray pulsed through deeper shades of magenta. Watching the play of pastel rainbow colors gave her the sense of a mother cradling her newborn. She witnessed the essence of pure joy. An almost imperceptible sensation accompanied it. As it grew in intensity, she felt the cells of her skin begin to tingle as if touched by feathery fingers of light. A power like an etheric vacuum gently lifted the debris from the old injury, transformed it in the pink light of her heart, and replaced it with new energy.

She realized she was on the outer edge of her heart looking at her newly restored solar plexus. She saw some of those earlier pink sparkles of light dancing over damaged areas of the grids. The transformation held her mesmerized. The tiny lights shifted to shimmering blue droplets, followed by the appearance of a blue grid. As the droplets hit the grid, some ignited and exploded. The energy disappeared into the glowing grid lines. Intuitively, she sent out a wave of love to ground and support them. It would take a while to manifest, but the changes were now in place. A sense of peace came to her. She closed her eyes and let herself be carried away in the flow.

***

With a slight jolt, Abe opened his eyes. They had been drifting on the waves of time and space for so long that he had let the fire go out. He tried to get up but felt a bit woozy. He laid back to re-ground himself. Not all of his bodies had made it back to the present, yet. When he opened his eyes again, he felt level-headed enough to stand up. He stirred the ashes to find some hot coals.

After raking a few together, he laid some twigs over them and soon had the fire burning brightly again. Then he laid back down to get some more sleep before sunrise. It wouldn't take long to surrender his body to Mother Earth's regenerating qualities. *We both need some help,* he thought, looking at his silent companion.

5. She Wakes Up

It took Abe several moments to remember where he was. Something had awakened him from a deep sleep, but what? His senses went on high alert — a groan? Then, he remembered his fellow companion. *Oh, my, I can't believe I forgot her!* He threw off his covers and almost tripped getting up. By the time he reached her side, she moaned again and reached up to the bandage on her head. She was still groggy, unaware of what had happened to her. She started mumbling to herself and then tried to get up.

"No, no, don't move," Abe told her gently. "Don't get up, yet." The strange voice seemed to bring her out of her dazed state. She blinked her eyes and then squinted to see who was there with her. "You've been hurt. I found you in a pit yesterday. Do you remember?"

She brought the face of the stranger into focus and stared into his eyes. He consciously and quietly met her gaze without speaking, giving her time to adjust to this strange situation. Time stood still. The brain fog hadn't cleared yet. He sensed her struggle to clear her head. He searched her eyes for a sign of recognition but wasn't prepared for such an intimate encounter. Her lovely, innocent eyes captured his soul in that unprotected moment. Her eyes were like an ocean he could swim in.

"Do you remember falling in the pit yesterday?" he asked again.

"Oh … Oh … Yes … Yes, now I'm remembering." She took some time to let her misadventure return to focus. He could see that she was getting her conscious mind back. "Who are you?" she finally asked in a husky voice.

"I am Abram, but most people call me Abe. What's your name?"

"I am Tythea of the Ry'el'na Clan. Everyone back home calls me Ty, or Ty'Yah. My younger brother couldn't say my name so he started calling me that, and it stuck."

"I like it."

"Thank you. Abe, I feel strange about asking this, but I need your help to relieve myself." It took him a moment to understand what she was trying to say. "Oh, oh, yes, sure. Sorry, I'm a little slow when it comes to being a caregiver.

"That's okay. You are going to have to be careful."

"I know." He helped her up and, before she could try to walk, he quickly picked her up, took her over by a thicket, and set her down on the smallest part of a log. He tested the firmness of the wood and decided it would support her. She pulled her tunic up and pulled her leggings down partially. He supported her while she pulled them lower and was ready to sit down on the limb. He turned to leave: "If you need any more help, call me, okay?" he said sternly.

"Yes, I will." Once she was done, she yelled, "Okay." He picked her up and returned to the pallet, but she stopped him before he could set her down. "No, no, I don't want to lie down. Help me over there on that big rock, please, if you don't mind."

"Are you sure? You had a nasty blow to your head, and your foot needs to be up."

"No, I'll be fine. If I need to lie down, I will, I promise."

"Okay, then."

Once she was comfortable, he went to stoke the fire. He had slept longer than he thought because there weren't any hot coals to be found. *I guess we needed the extra sleep,* he thought. *I told my body that I didn't want to wake up at its normal time.* Before long, he had the fire burning brightly again.

She watched him as he went down to the creek, fetched some water, and set the pot by the fire. She realized she enjoyed watching this stranger work. There was something about him she couldn't quite put her finger on. *I feel so comfortable and safe with him. It's as if I already know him.* Once he had water heating, she informed him that she had some herbs in her bag for tea.

"Yes, I found them last night."

"How did you know that?"

"Because I had to assess what you had. I had to clean you up last night and had to figure out what I had to eat. Some of those herbs came in handy for your injuries."

"So, you know your herbs, then?"

"Yes, to a certain extent. I know enough to get by. I'm sure I don't know them like you do, though," he grinned.

"How do you know that?"

"Because you have way more than I would have. You have so many that you must know how to use them all."

"Well, you're right there. It is one of my great loves. It all comes so naturally to me. I come from a long line of healers. I have to say it is one of my gifts that I enjoy the most."

"That's great."

"Can you please bring the pouch over, so I can show you what to put in my tea?"

"Sure." He picked up the overstuffed pouch and handed it to her. She thumbed through different bags and picked out three.

"They'll help with my pain and my healing. And, if you don't mind, make it strong so I can drink it throughout the day?"

"Sure, sure." He worked quietly, preparing their food. She sipped on her hot tea as he went back for another wooden bowl. "Is the tea helping?"

"Yes, I can feel my pain easing up." As they ate, she started thinking about their situation. "What are we going to do?"

"Well, I was waiting to see how you were doing before we talked about that. How do you feel?"

"Oh, I feel pretty good, I guess. As good as you can expect with a bum leg, a headache, and this gash on my head. But other than that, I feel good," she grinned. He liked her sense of humor.

"Back to the question of what to do," she said. She noticed that he seemed to be reluctant and was selecting his words with caution.

"I am assuming …" he hesitated, "that you came to this forest for the same reason I did. Is that correct?"

"I came because of many visions, as well as a prophecy I must fulfill. I was directed to go on a quest and find Zathera."

"I as well," Abe admitted. "I have been here for several weeks now, getting to know the terrain around the old Village, some from my own experiences, but mainly from my mother's visions. She was a seer and had many dreams about this place over her lifetime." He felt feelings beginning to resurface as he talked about her. His voice started to quiver as he talked about the circumstances surrounding his departure and then told her some of what happened last night.

As he related their out-of-body experiences, she noticed some strange memories starting to come to the surface. Another dense fog seemed to be lifting. She put to work some of her dream retrieval techniques to capture those unconscious images. By the time Abe finished his story, she felt as if she had remembered what she needed to know. She quietly assimilated what he had shared. "I am so sorry for your loss and that you had to leave your mother at that time."

"Thanks."

"I know it would also be weird for me to leave just before my mother's passing. Truthfully, I don't know if I could do it. Why would you, especially when you would normally want to help with her death rites?" She hoped he knew what she was referring to.

"Oh, yes, it was the hardest thing I've ever done. But, after understanding where she was coming from, I felt I had to." He chuckled. "She would have no part of me staying. When she felt something that strongly, you just had to listen because her wisdom was always spot on. She helped me to understand why I had to leave immediately, and I agreed, even though my brain said otherwise. It was a test. This was another chance for me to learn to trust her guidance and go with it. Now I understand that she wanted to be free to work with me from the other side when I arrived at Zathera."

"She sounds like she was an amazing woman. I would have liked to have known her.

Yes, you would have liked her, he told her intuitively.

Tythea was silent for a moment, and then, out of the blue, she said: "Abe, tell me about the ruins, the dwellings you said you found. Tell me all about them."

"Well, at this point, what can I say? If I tell you what I've seen, you won't believe me. I know because I wouldn't have either. All I can say for now is you will feel like you have come home, and you will have many more questions than I'll have answers for. That's what I've come to know for myself. It is a very mysterious place, I can tell you."

"I can't wait. When can we go? How far away is it? How long will it take?"

"Wow, slow down a bit. I need to explain one of the many mysteries about this place before we go any further. I've learned it the hard way, and in some ways, you'll have to, also. Maybe it won't have to be as hard for you because I can warn you ahead of time. It took me a couple of days to work my way to the center. Zathera is the center of this realm, this mountain range. I call it a realm because it's not like anything I've ever seen outside of here.

It's like living on another planet, or in a different dimension, but it's here and tangible, if you can shift your old way of thinking."

6. A Summary of the Rings

"I grew up hearing my mother's stories about the energy around Zathera. She described it as a golden dome of Light that covered the whole mountain: an energy dome within an energy dome within an energy dome, five of them in all. Each of these domed realms represented the evolution of a layer of the human experience. As you know, we have evolved through four layers. The dead zone is the first, or what many call the spirit world. Then the physical, emotional, and mental worlds. The fifth is the center, the village itself.

I call them energy bands, or Rings, that surround the Sacred Mountain. You will have to go through each of them to reach the fifth, which is in the center where the Village is located, what we call the "Mystery School." These rings protect the Mysteries from the outer kingdoms. No one can enter unless they can pass the tests, which decontaminate them from negativity. In a sense, it's like a labyrinth of rings. Do you know what that is?"

"Yes, I do."

"You have to stay focused and honest with yourself if you are to reach the center. My mother explained that these energy zones correspond to the different levels of density in the body. In our first evolutionary state, the Earth was still very young and very warm. Universally, all life forms are required to stay in balance with their environment. Consequently, we had very little density under those conditions. At first, all of the human family lived in harmony. Gradually, however, a desire took root in a few of us to separate our lives from the rest of the family. That eventually tipped the balance to the point that conflict arose and the old world ended. The few remaining survivors now found themselves with an additional body that took them deeper into density. This created a new dimension on Earth that matched their frequency. At this point, civilization started all over again. This was the 2nd earth, represented by the second ring. This scenario repeated a second and third time — the 3rd and 4th rings — as we descended into density until we reached our present form. Once inside each layer, you must face your unresolved genetic issues at that frequency level. Each one represents an energetic body that evolved after separation.

"The outer Ring we're in now relates to the dead zone. When I first entered it, I started seeing spirits who looked like me. I recognized some of my relatives. They wouldn't leave me alone.

It was almost impossible to sleep. I couldn't do anything until I started putting all of my memories of them together, and then a common theme emerged. I had to confront the fact that we carried a strong, judgmental ego. I don't think I've ever experienced such darkness in me. Like we've heard in the old stories, this is a scary place, and now I know why. It felt as if a boulder was lifted off my chest when all of that anxiety and pressure was finally released. It was as if I could breathe again. Any questions before I go on to the next one?"

"So, you're telling me that I will have to face my unresolved issues when I cross through that ring of energetics?"

"Yes. You will come face-to-face with the subconscious demons that your ancestors created that are still lurking in the shadows. That ring will lift the veil hiding them so you can see them for what they are. A spiritual journey starts in darkness but leads to the light of your Indwelling presence."

"In other words, to have a balanced inner life, my shadows must be brought into the light.

"Yes. Well put."

It took a while for her to absorb this. "Okay, go on."

"The second zone took me deeper into the old belief patterns that I inherited. These take on the form of sub-personalities that live as egos, judging right from wrong and telling you what to do. I saw clusters of different energies that had fed them down through time. Number one seems to deal with subpersonalities. In the second circle, you actually perceive the energy behind your negative thoughts and see the energy you created. They will manifest as the strong judgments you've projected on other people. Remember, we've decided to wake up so we have to take an honest look at everything that we've created unknowingly. Then, we can decide what to do with anything that is not beneficial."

"Well," Ty said, "one of the ways I was taught was how to recycle them. It's so much better to thank them for their service and recycle them rather than simply killing them off.

Relieve them of their negative charge and assign them a useful job so they can evolve along with us. Those egos had to stand in for us until we were ready to wake up and be present in our bodies."

"Exactly," Abe said, as he continued. "All of our limitations that we have given life to need to be weeded out. We need to recognize what is beneficial and what is not.

Ty raised a finger. "I like a description my gramps uses. He was our family's archivist. He would always go back and edit everything that he wrote. He said that he was editing his thoughts, and that term always stayed with me. I like it," Ty said. "Sorry. Go ahead. I didn't mean to interrupt."

"It's okay. Over the last few weeks, I've had a lot of time to examine my feelings and think about what I've experienced. I've found that another way to understand these energy bands is to see them as reflections of our unconscious. Our nightmares come from our unconscious mind. It's a scary place, but we must have the courage to go in there if we wish to wake up to who we really are, right? Since separation, we have not been conscious of how we're living. That's called 'being asleep.' As a species, we don't remember how to be responsible for our thoughts and actions, if we ever knew it. It's been bred out of us as a culture, one generation after another."

"Yes, we can be clueless about all of the unseen energies that we carry around as useless traits and habitual memories that take us over, even possess some people." She slapped her hand over her mouth once she realized what she had just said. "I apologize," she chuckled. "You can see it's a pet peeve of mine, irresponsible people. I know its ignorance, but it seems like some people don't want to learn."

"Yes, I know what you mean." He shook his head and grinned: "Exactly."

He continued. "While I was in that band, I also saw the grid there. It had several intersections covered with a black, tar-like ooze, which seemed to be dripping onto the grid layers below. Images with black heads rose through the tar, their loud voices echoing in my head, and they wouldn't shut up. It could drive you crazy if you aren't careful."

"Gees, that sounds really scary."

"It is if you don't understand what's going on. Those grids are a metaphor that refers to our awakening. They are the place of our fears that stand in our way. We are responsible for that energy."

"I've never heard of anything like these protective rings. It's all so strange," she said. I'm still not accustomed to the idea that this sacred mountain is protected by these outer rings, but it's a good symbol of what it takes to discover our divine potential. It is a masterful design. I've already learned a lot about myself in the brief time I've been here searching for the entrance. Now that's a perfect symbol. Oh, here I go again."

"What do you mean?" he frowned.

"Well, it just dawned on me that the doorway to this mountain is a symbol of the doorway we have to find to our inner kingdom."

"Oh, I see where you're going. Yes. Yes. They both have to line up, the inner and the outer doors. Also, the same with the surface self and the inner self. First, the outer surface, you that I'm talking to, is learning to recognize that there is something inside that is divine, right? Then, you discover that your inner self is aware of your universal spirit, your omnipresence. This is called 'Awakening.'"

"Yes," she said with a big smile. We each discover our own master teacher who can help us to see the dangers of our negative egos. You have a way for the surface self and the divine self to talk to each other. It's great how it's all coming together."

She went on. "Now, back to the doorway. At first, your whole life is focused on what is outside of you until there's a moment when you're not doing anything, and your attention is captured by something like a beautiful sunset, for example, and at that moment, a quiet voice speaks inside of you. The more it speaks to you, the more you open up to a new, inner life, which will lead you to the door of your heart and, if you knock on that door, it will open to your inner source. I can see that, in the future, anyone who finds this sacred door will be initiated into the rites of this mountain. Wow! You are right. This place metaphorically represents our spiritual journey — it's like a map. Oh, I led us off the topic, didn't I?"

"In a way, but not really," he smiled. "Those were some great insights."

"Yeah, I thought so, too. It was neat how it all pieced together. Go ahead. Lead on."

"Do you have a sense of the second ring now?

"Yes, I think so. It's more about the mental imagery that's behind everything our thoughts create, especially those negative programs. We need to understand how our psyche can create egos when we experience something traumatic. Egos are born out of trauma. I know I'm putting some of my own understanding in here but we need to be able to see that these ego personalities are not truly us."

"Yes, that's perfect. Ready for the third band?"

"Yes, go ahead."

"It relates more to our emotional body and all of its suppressed trauma and trapped genetic baggage. It is a 2-step process. The first step is to uncover all of those feelings that have been denied and pushed down into the lower parts of the body. These come from the sensitive, more feminine side of our nature. The counterpart is the mental body with its tendency to judge everything, which is more of a masculine characteristic. This often leads to conflict and a tendency of the mental life to deny and control the emotional life. From the beginning of duality, the emotional life has been suppressed, especially for women who display it. You must understand how these affect your life to pass through this band. After identifying these suppressed characteristics, the final step is to release them. This retarding energy must be confronted, cleared, and balanced to pass through this plane. Success here depends on being honest and open with yourself. Here I felt a lot of discomfort in my body as it tried to show me where stuff was stuck. I learned to listen to any and every pain I felt. That was new for me. Don't get me wrong; I've felt my body before, but never like this."

"This is good to know. Thanks."

"Okay," Abe continued, "the fourth relates to the current physical body and the changes we're going through. It is about metamorphosis. Our body is in a cocoon stage. I didn't notice much at first. Where I experienced it the most was in my lower half: lower gut, muscle spasms, and joint discomfort. Then it became more difficult. I started feeling heavy, and at one point, I felt as if I was buried alive, unable to move. Trapped. I know, now, how the body felt after it was hijacked and forced to carry all of this genetic garbage. I had to work through feelings of hopelessness and depression."

"The invaders wanted us to work under their control, but they didn't want us to thrive, so they disconnected most of our life forces. Our ability to move forward was lost. Instead of a life that flows freely, we often encounter obstacles that we would rather dodge, giving us a tendency to deny them. Denial leads to avoidance and repression. Movement must be restored for healing to occur. I heard this from my mother, and the rings really brought it home

"In some ways, I've started experiencing that, too," she told him. "Well, I guess it's my turn. Thanks for the heads up."

"Did you recognize the old ruins at the entrance to the stone circle, above the waterfall?" he asked.

"Oh, yes, I did. I was warned about that old circle."

"Did you notice any discomfort as you meandered through the maze?"

"I sure did. I had to stop to realign myself several times to make it through because I kept getting disoriented," she said. There was a pained expression on her face. "I don't know how long it took me to get through the gateway."

"Energetically, I think this mountain is one gigantic labyrinth," he went on to say. "You know, as I was putting into words what I experienced through the rings, I realized something. Helping you is also healing my own feminine side that I've been cut off from. I've already been through this once for myself, but now we're doing it together, and that is important. I'll be helping you as you go through it, and you'll be helping me. The collective will also benefit from everything we do here. Wow, I'm beginning to see the bigger picture! Does this make any sense?" He placed his hands on his abdomen. "I can feel it here. Can you?"

"Yes, yes, I do. I do," she told him. "Is this new for you?"

He was quiet. "Yes, it is. I don't usually feel stuff in my lower body. How did you know?"

"Well," she smiled, "it's not new for me. That's where I feel the most, here, in my upper diaphragm.

"Well, something has changed in me. Do you think something new has been activated in me since I've been here?"

"It sure sounds like it. It doesn't surprise me."

"I thought so," he said, a little puzzled. "Now, to change the subject, here's the next question. Do you think you are up to the challenge today, or shall we just hang out here for another day, and head on tomorrow? Do you need another day to rest is what I'm asking."

She closed her eyes to ask her body consciousness. She felt that she might be able to make it, but she decided to wait for a while and see. Because he would be carrying her, she would be okay. "How long will it take to get there? I know you said it depends on how fast I can process the different levels. Can we get there by dark? But I guess we could camp, if need be, and proceed in the morning."

"Right. Okay, we have a plan then. You let me know when you feel you can leave."

"Sure. So, Abe, why were you in the woods yesterday and not at the ruins? How did you happen to be way out here on the outer rim?"

"Well, it wasn't until after I heard you calling that I knew why. That's when I understood why my guidance had me out running around. I thought I was just out exploring since I enjoy it so much. I was also curious about the area around Zathera. I guess there was more than one reason. It's funny how that always works out."

"What do you mean?"

"Let me explain that a little better. I meant that there always seems to be more than one reason for everything. I guess I was to explore the woods so that I would be around to hear you. Last night, until I talked with my Mother, I was puzzled about why you would need to have this so-called accident. But when she explained what she saw, I understood better."

"Oh, okay, I get it. But I still don't understand why I needed all of this?" as she put her hand on her bandaged head.

He had to chuckle. "I apologize. It's a long story, but I guess we've got the time, don't we?

"Okay, but if it's that long, I need to get a softer seat. My butt's going to sleep on me. I think I'd better get back over on my pallet."

He helped her get up and then swung her into his arms. His action caught her off guard. Before she knew it, he had crossed the short distance and was putting her down. He could see how startled she was.

"I didn't think you would let me pick you up without complaining. You have to take it easy, and I can see you don't always listen very well. You aren't that heavy for me so don't be concerned. It isn't an inconvenience for me, okay?"

"Okay, you're right: I would have complained and would have fussed about it.

"I can tell you are used to being on the other side. You haven't been a patient much, have you?" He grinned.

"No, you're right. I can see I needed that lesson."

"You see, we need to talk about this because how are we going to get to the Dwellings if I don't carry you? Plus, you shouldn't try to walk on that leg for a few days; you've got a bad sprain. And, since I am making a list here, you have a head injury, too."

"Okay, okay, I get the point, I hear you. You're right. I'll let you carry me."

He helped her sit down and turned to re-stoke the fire. As she sat there looking back over what had just happened, she noticed she was still feeling his arms under her.

***

He put me down, so why am I feeling him? She took several deep breaths and put the question to her body consciousness. Her body knew his touch from some past experience. The prospect of being carried by him for a long distance had stirred up something deep in her body, and she willed it to calm down. *There is something taking place between us, but I just haven't had time to process it all, consciously. Yes, I remember some hazy dream scenarios, but what I feel the most is something I have no words for yet.* She could feel both his strength and his tenderness. Like a breaching whale, her next realization shot up so fast that it almost caught her off guard again. *He's the one!* The thought came as a shock at first, but as it faded away, a sense of peace took its place. *I have found him, the one in my dreams.*

She placed her hands over her heart and began to breathe in the awareness of it. It was the key she needed to unlock those old memories that hadn't completely surfaced yet. All that had happened now stood before her. The clouds quickly rolled away, and she saw into his very soul.

***

She watched him wash their bowls and repack everything. He poured her tea into her water container and went to refill his own. He had everything almost ready to leave.

Abe needed the time to process how she was affecting him. After he was done cleaning up, he said, "I'm going to go pick some plums. The thicket's not too far away. Are you okay while I go get some for our trip?"

"Yes, I'm fine for now."

"Good. Now take this time to get a little rest while I'm gone."

"Okay."

"We'll talk when I get back."

Before long, she opened her eyes and realized she had fallen asleep. He had just placed some wood on the fire, which woke her up.

"Oh, sleepy head, you finally woke up."

"I went to sleep," she said in a fog.

"Yes, when I got back, you were gone."

"How long was I out?"

"Oh, long enough for the fire to almost go out again."

"Oh, I didn't want to go to sleep. We need to leave, soon, don't we?"

"We could. How are you feeling now that you have had some rest?"

"I feel better. Before I went to sleep, I had an experience, and I think it helped me shift my energy. I thought over our morning and retraced all that I experienced. It was as if a huge cloud was lifted off of me, and I remembered much more of what happened when I was unconscious. It was as if I had this long dream. What I'm saying is it seemed like both a dream and a reality. You get my point?"

"Yes, I do."

"I needed the rest to help process what happened dimensionally. My energy level is so much better now. I feel I am ready to go, that is, if you're still ready to carry me. And my head feels much clearer now, so I can do my inner work as we go. I realize that, up until now, I wasn't ready to go yet."

"Great." He stood up and started gazing into her field, quietly assessing her health and strength. He finally agreed with her. "You are much clearer and better aligned than you were earlier. Your bodies are re-integrating nicely, but I think we need to wait a little while longer and then see how you feel, okay?" He sat down on the log across from her. Ty asked him to tell her how he got her out of the old pit. "I need your help to put it all into perspective from an awakened state. I think I remember for the most part, but it feels like one of my dreams. For you, it's conscious. I need to know what's real and what's not. Will you help me?"

"Sure. We have nothing but time. Zathera will be there when we get there."

He told her everything he had experienced since he heard her first faint cry for help and how he brought her here. He told her about remembering his last few days with his Mother, and when she reappeared to him to tell him she had passed on.

"I'm sorry for your loss. That would be hard for me to do. I feel for you."

"Thank you."

"So, what happened after your mother told you that we had work to do together?"

"She said that she had never seen a field like yours, that you were very special."

"I guess she encouraged you and let you know that I was okay. I need to thank her for that." She smiled shyly.

"So, do you remember anything about last night?" he finally asked.

"Well, from the little I've picked up on, it felt like I did some time traveling of sorts. Is that true?"

"You could call it that," he said with a big, knowing smile.

A memory came to mind. "I remember a feeling of flying," she said. I felt like a bird flying at a high rate of speed above a grid. Suddenly, I hit a wall and couldn't go any farther." She felt herself getting lightheaded and focused on her breathing to keep from getting pulled back into her unconscious experience. Intuitively, she knew she needed more clarity about that experience.

"Anything else?" he probed cautiously.

"I remember my mother and father smiling at me. Wait!" she said excitedly, "We went back in time and visited the Mother and Father God of this reality."

That brought Abe back their whole experience. He didn't say anything.

"What's wrong?" she asked.

"Oh, nothing. I'm just speechless. I can't believe you remember. I'm shocked."

"What can I say?" she smiled. "I have a very active dream life. I can remember everything that happened. I come from a long line of seers on both sides. But, of course, all of us Zatherians have amazing gifts like this, don't we?"

"Yes, we do. It stands to reason because we remember our divine birthright, which endowed us with these abilities. So, what would you say is your family's primary gift to the collective?"

"Well, as I said, the divine integrated dreamer."

"How would you describe it? If I were a newbie, how would you explain it to me? What makes it different from the so-called normal dreamer? And, why is there a difference between the two?"

She was quiet for a while. "Can you bring your dreams across the bridge as you wake up, the bridge between sleeping and waking? Can you see how they relate to your waking life? You know, a normal person dreams from the egoic archetypes that were created after separation. These imps, if you will, write your dream scenarios. They send you messages that can help you sometimes, but in fact, they reflect your daily life and are fueled by your subconscious mind. Your dreams come out of this energy pool of unresolved issues."

"Personally," she continued, "I don't want this kind of dreaming, especially now that I know the difference. The divine dreamer can be consciously activated once you begin to wake up to your innate potential. At this point, you want a different messaging system, a different guidance, one that's free of egos, fear, and guilt. To be a divine dreamer means you've created a sacred space within your heart that allows you to reorganize those old egoic constructs. This subconscious system was set up to help store and compartmentalize repressed emotions, denials, and fears. This old process has to be switched over to a new, more conscious, and aware processing system, which resurrects and activates an ancient connection that has been turned off in your omnipresent mind. Once this comes to life, a new, divine dreamer is born."

Ty continued, "When you open your spark chamber within your heart, your dreams will become a reliable source of guidance and understanding. You will be able to change old karmic patterns because you're willing to consciously look at yourself and learn more about who you are."

"Give me an example, if you don't mind," Abe said.

"My parents explained that the old dreamer was designed to put you in contact with other people who had signed contracts with you."

"How's that?" Abe looked puzzled.

"Well, 'contracts' means you both need to learn from the same lesson. Think about it, Abe. When you are asleep, you can't learn your lessons through observation."

"True."

"So, you need other people to be able to learn. As my granny said, there is this big, woven fabric that represents everything that is going to happen in your life. It's woven before you are born from all of the genetic programming from which you chose to make your body. Everything is on it, all of your unresolved emotions, all of your unfinished thoughts, your actions. It's all there. The only way to change that fabric is to heal something. That happens at night. The dreamer can re-weave it and reset the grid for the next three days. This dream grid is written according to what is resolved in your genetics."

"Here are a couple more examples. This old dreamer ultimately created the 'victim' role, allowing one person to blame another for their own mistakes. The dream shows you that 'X' did something to you, so 'X' is the problem, but 'X' is really you. Another aspect is believing in karma and that there are bills to pay and lessons to learn, which is true. But when this belief rules your life, then the external becomes your teacher, not the internal. The internal dynamics are about you learning to observe other people's lives so that you don't have to experience the trauma for yourself. Having your eyes wide open allows you to learn from every direction, learning instantly through understanding, meaning you don't have to have the drama of pain to learn. Choosing to be awake and aware in every moment dissolves the need for contracts. It's the resistance that has created the need for lessons like these. Did I answer your questions?"

"Yes," Abe replied. "Now, explain more about the new dreamer you were talking about."

"Okay, after someone begins to perceive the inner dynamics and opens up a sacred space to contain this new system, it can be ignited. This resurrects the omnipresent mind. The mind links with your spiritual genetics, and now you have a way to exist on the other side. Your mind can then use your new dreamer to show you how to wake up, be conscious, and understand what's going on in your body."

"So, the bridge is you reopening this circuit, connecting both sides again?"

"Yes."

Abe pondered that for a moment. "Hmm. This brings back a dream I had a long time ago when my mother was working with me around dreaming. I wonder if it was trying to show me my bridge. There was a beautiful rainbow that stretched across a really wide canyon, right in front of my feet. It was so beautiful that I knew I would never forget it."

"It sure sounds like it," Ty said. "It reminds me of one I had that was very similar."

Abe sat in quiet thought again. "I do get it. I guess part of myself might fall into the normal dreamer category since I wasn't exactly conscious of what you just explained."

"I don't know that I would automatically say that. I would need more information about your method, first."

"It sure sounds like you have more understanding around this than I do. But, on second thought, I do receive messages from my inner source, just like you do. I'll share my family's strongest gift. Then you might understand where I'm coming from. We called them waking journeys."

"I like the name," Ty said. Tell me more."

"I go into a meditative, semi-trance state while still conscious and travel through my sacred space. Someone once told me that I was an astral traveler, but I call it divine astral journeys. That's what I call it now. My way isn't astral traveling because I don't go out of the top of my head like they probably do. I go through my inner source like I know you do. It looks like we both have achieved two different modes of traveling through the heart," he said, placing his hands over his chest. "We understand the importance of our sacred heart channel. I don't have the silver cord that they talk about because I experimented with it a couple of times with my mother's help. Nothing happened. We assumed it was because I hadn't created the belief that everything was outside of me. I think we both know our protection comes from the heart method."

"It sounds like we are on the same wavelength," she told him.

"Ty, did you finish what you were saying? Go ahead with what you were going to explain.

7. The Divine Dreamer

"Oh, yeah, okay. My journeys are so unique because I have achieved a way to contact my twin," Ty said.

"Twin?"

"Yes, the twin that stayed on the other side after separation."

"Oh, I got you. I see where you're going. You mean your omnipresent mind."

"Yes, our original twin aspect, our original light body that was forced to remain on another plane after separation. So, you learned about this?"

"Yes," Abe replied, "our family talked about this."

"Good. Well, it's this light body that I'm talking about. We must consciously open a communication channel to receive input from our twin selves. Then, we must switch our egoic dreamer over to the divine dreamer. By doing this, we can receive much clearer messages to apply to our waking life."

"So, the bridge brings these two twin aspects together?"

"Yes. I call it a bridge because it allows us to communicate with that part of ourselves, which was cut off from us up until now. This is what sets our dreams apart from so-called normal dreams."

"Right," Abe said, listening intently. "Go on."

"Okay. Step one is to understand that it's up to each of us to create this communication link. We must take the initiative. It comes down to loving every part of ourselves, but sometimes it seems like there's a war going on between one part and another." She threw her hands up in the air in a gesture of surrender. "Put up a flag of truce."

"Good point."

"Right now, our four bodies, physical, emotional, mental, and spiritual, are being held in solitary confinement. What can we do? How can we re-script our genetics? A new space must be opened inside, right?"

"Yes," he said.

"And from where?"

"From in here," he said, tapping his chest. "Your heart."

"Yes. Our four bodies have been programmed to keep to themselves, so there's no innate way to love your body. This awakening means that you must recognize the importance of loving your physical body instead of judging or criticizing it. This is you; your spiritual genetics are waking up."

"Step two: open up a sacred space in your heart in order for your body to have the experience of being loved. The heart is supposed to be all about love, right? Separation created the illusion of duality, right and wrong, good and bad. The body had to be brought under control, rather than loved. We had to avoid breaking the law. If not, we were sinners, but I chose a different attitude. I see myself as standing in front of my heart's door. I choose to go through that door, go back inside myself, and embrace the person that I am — all of me."

"I got it," Abe said.

"The first time you walk through that door, you're in a strange place. You have to search in the dark to locate your inner light, the spiritual spark of your life. Until that moment, that innocent life is in an unconscious, dormant state. It is up to each one to find it and re-awaken it to consciousness."

"I've got to rant a bit here. Why is it so hard to believe that you are beautiful and amazing? You are a being with the intelligence and power to create your own life and wake up to the divine life within you. It's there within each one of us. Why would anyone choose to ignore this miracle? It's beyond me," she said as she slapped her good leg. "It just boggles my mind that people can't perceive their divine potential. This spark shows you where you touch your indwelling god. Once this is fully comprehended, you then have a right to manifest those divine aspects and set them around your inner campfire, so to speak. Now, you have a council formed out of your spiritually evolved physical, emotional, mental, and spiritual bodies. You want the most highly evolved, aware aspects to come forward. Invite them in and welcome them back home, not to rule but to communicate with each other as a working group. Treat them all as equals, so they all feel safe. Each can express themselves on any issue in a loving, compassionate, and understanding way. All parts of yourself can grow and thrive in this space."

"Why the visual of a council fire?" he asked.

"Because fire is an image of warmth and light that shares itself equally with all. It is a symbol of comfort and peace. It is the center in which all parts of yourself are at home and welcomed. It is an image of sacredness. With this understanding, your omnipresence can now make use of this new guidance system, your divine dreamer. My parents taught me most of this. Use this tool in your meditations, and it will set the stage for personal transformation. Also, remember that it's your personal, divine spark that has the authority to delete and rewrite the old genetic codes."

"That makes sense," Abe said. "I never thought of all that. I like the part about the twin and the bridging work you talked about. I'll add it to my inner work. It feels good."

"I'm sure, in your own way, it's already a part of you. I can't see how it could be otherwise, because you are here. When you believe in your inner source, then your omnipresence automatically comes with it."

"I have another question."

"Okay, shoot."

Abe paused for a moment. "I know how I'm still reeling from the download last night. How are you dealing with it so far? I know you weren't consciously aware of it until just now. How are you able to handle so much energy?"

"Well, she said as she put her hands over her belly, first it's taken me a long time to learn how to hold my heart focus on more than one level at a time. I guess it ultimately came out of creating this dimensional relationship with my twin, along with all my bodies."

"How do you mean?"

"Well, it's like the example you gave of how to go through the different zones here to reach the village. It's really the same thing, but it's all an inward process. My parents taught me a lot about dreaming, but this key came out of my own inner teacher, my omnipresence. It gave me a very clear message through a dream, which took me a while to bring to life in me."

"Are you going to tell me what he showed you?"

"Sure, if you want. I was shown a door that opened onto two levels. The first was an overgrown doorway that needed to be cleaned up if it was to be used again. Once I got the door completely cleared, I opened it and walked through it. I felt each step I took as if I were reopening closed circuits in my body. That process took me to the next door. I soon learned why. All of our bodies want to come together in a unified consciousness so that they don't feel left out. All of them want to ascend as one, cohesive package. I learned that my body remembers a time when it was whole. That's what it showed me. I understand this now, but it took me a while to get it through my head." She patted her head. "As you said, it's hard for the head to perceive what the body feels, but if it's the truth, then this feeling will trigger a chemical change that will alter our genetic codes. You remember how I had to clean up around that first door before I could open it?"

"Yes."

"You, the individual, must change your thoughts and beliefs if you want to change your genetics. The overgrown genetic brush and brambles have blocked the door to your inner source. I had to clear generational negative programming to enter that door. Once on the other side, I saw the next door up ahead, which brought all of those aspects back together. This switched out the old egoic writer with the new divine guidance system. With that, my dreams changed almost overnight, and so did my outer life. This also activated many more dimensional levels in my dream life. As I learned this, I shared it with my parents, and they noticed a whole new world opened up for them as well. Unconditional love is the key; it's the miracle that unlocks new levels in you. It's what ends all of your inner struggles."

She went on. "My parents also taught me how to observe my waking life as if it were a dream. Have you heard of this?"

"No, I don't think so. Give me an example so I can see what you mean."

After a pause, she said: "Okay, I got it. We'll use my falling into that hole as an example. Why did you hear me, and why would you need to save me? That was a daydream. Why did it happen to you? How would you interpret the symbolism? What understanding do you need to get out of this?"

Abe thought for a second. "Well, there are many things that happened out of that."

"Yes. Do you get what I am trying to say? It's a way of being aware of what you're attracting into your waking life. I've learned it's just as important as your dreams. Messages can come from both sides, so you can learn from everything. You can also watch someone else's life lesson and learn how to or how not to live your own life just from observing them. In that way, everyone can become a teacher for you."

"Very true," he said. "I think I understand. I will have to put that to work. Wow, we've had quite a discussion here, but now, we need to figure out what to do, because if we don't go, we won't get back before it gets dark. It's even later than I like. We'll have to really push it." He felt a bit stressed. "How are you feeling?"

"Oh, I feel pretty good."

"Do you feel level-headed enough now?"

"Yes."

"You check, and I'll recheck your bandage." Once convinced that she was fine, Abe decided they could leave. He rolled her blanket up, doused the hot coals with water, and swung the packs over his shoulder.

"You ready?" He picked her up as if she were a leaf.

"I can't believe how easily you pick me up like I'm a rag doll or something," she chuckled, "and I've never been involved with someone as a full equal. They always seemed so, I don't know, spiritually immature. In just a short time, we've shared so much and found out we have a lot in common."

How fitting, Abe thought, *that they were destined to be together on every level.* She smiled and looked up into his face. He stopped and asked if she was comfortable.

"Yes, thank you," she told him with a slightly shaky voice. She laid her head against his chest, against his rapidly beating heart.

After several moments of carefully choosing where to step, he finally reached a wider trail. He felt her body relax. He felt their heartbeats tuning into the rhythm.

Ty's body relaxed as she fell into a shallow sleep.

Their movement became more of a challenge, pushing through the boulder-strewn forest path. He was grateful for the thick stand of oak and chestnut that allowed for hardly any underbrush. He finally allowed himself to play with the notion that drifted in and out of his thoughts: what would it feel like to kiss those red, beautiful lips? He could almost feel them. *Why is it so strong?* he asked himself. *It's as if I remember how they feel.* He replayed his feelings being with her, and what his mother had said. He now knew Ty to be the one he had been waiting for. This brought him a sense of peace. They had been together before, many times in fact, according to his intuition. *All in good time. I will kiss them again when it feels right.* With this decision, he turned his attention back to the old animal path he was following.

He couldn't believe how many stones and trees he had to skirt around. Finally, he began to feel the influences of the next band of energy. He needed to re-attune himself if he was going to pass through it again. Within seconds, he shifted his internal frequency to align with this ring. He knew that she would be waking up at any moment. Even in her sleep, she would feel the pressure rising. Right on cue, her beautiful eyes popped open, delighting him again. As she blinked, the dark fog lifted, and she realized where she was.

"I fell asleep, again," she half-apologized.

"Yes, you've had a good nap. You woke up just in time." Before he could say another word, she started making a face.

"What's going on?" she asked, a frown forming on her lips.

"Well, I was about to warn you that we're reaching the next ring." He set her down on a large boulder ahead of them.

"Yes, that will be fine. I'm sure you're ready to get some rest of your own."

"Yes, my arms and shoulders could use a rest, even though I enjoyed carrying you," he smiled." They looked at each other, and Abe noticed a faint smile on her lips and a twinkle in her eyes.

***

As they continued on, she noticed that there was a moment of hesitation in his stride, and she intuited that he had almost stopped to kiss her. It was so strong that she wanted to reach up and bring his lips down to her own, but before she could, he looked back at the trail as he approached a dry, washed-out creek bed. *He needs his full attention to wind his way around the maze of stone*, she thought. She knew in her heart of hearts that they were ancient lovers with a long history together. A deep ache stirred in her bones to bring that history back to life again. Their love and respect for each other represented a never-ending saga. Where would their future take them this time? She resolved that if a moment arose like this again, she would act on how she felt. A buildup of abdominal pressure needed her attention. She asked him to set her down so she could focus on her breathing. I'm feeling bad abdominal pain." She realized that she had some vibrational stuff to take care of. This allowed him to walk off into the woods to relieve himself.

"There's a nearby patch of berries that my elemental friends led me to when I first came up the mountain. I'm going to grab us some," Abe called out to Ty.

She watched a flock of little sparrows fly up to pinpoint the location. Their noisy chatter let her know that they enjoyed the succulent feast. Abe gave an offering to the earth and filled his bag with the berries.

She was waiting for him after finishing her exercise. "Look what I found." He put a bulging cloth carefully in her hands, folding back the corners to reveal the big juicy berries. She teased him about how red his lips looked.

"How would you know that?"

"Your mouth, silly."

"Oh, yes, I enjoyed a bunch, too."

She ate them slowly and savored the elemental energy. "Life begets life," she told the berries. "I recognize it in you, and you recognize it in me. Together we are one. Thank you. Thanks for thinking of me."

"You are welcome," he bowed playfully.

After she finished, she informed him that she needed to visit the bush, as well. He picked her up and took her outside the stone outcropping and left her there. "I'm done," she called out. He brought her back and checked the placement of her bandages on her head and her foot. They snacked on some bread from her bag.

"Ready to proceed?" he asked.

"The question should be, are you rested enough?" she asked him.

"Me? Sure, this is nothing. Carrying you is easy work. I enjoy it."

She noticed from his expression that his words surprised him. He seemed a little embarrassed. *Like me, he's not used to being in a relationship.* His clumsiness at this sort of thing mirrored the way she felt. "Whenever you're ready, I am ready," she told him.

He offered her one last swallow of water, returned the container to its place, and swung her up in his arms. Their eyes locked, and Ty knew this was the moment. He hesitated. *Oh, silly, you don't have to wait on him.* She reached for his head, but he was already leaning toward her lips. As their lips touched, their reality collapsed into that sensual moment. This new feeling of tender surrender captured her heart. She sensed he reacted the same way. Reluctantly, they pulled apart.

"Wow! Woman, what you do to me!"

"Yes, I feel it, too," she whispered, not yet back from the place she slipped into. She willed for that part of herself to stay present rather than slip away. *I know it was heavenly, but the kiss is over. We have plenty of time to experience it again.* She breathed deeply as she held his gaze.

"On we must go," Abe said as he stole one more quick kiss. She noticed him having to breathe deeply himself as he returned to the trail. A thicket of small trees forced him to duck and weave his way through.

As they headed towards the next invisible field, he asked her what she had experienced when they stopped. She told him that her barometer went off to indicate that new energy had entered her heart's spark chamber. "I seem to be multidimensional there." She made a quirky frown. "It always goes off when something new comes in, and it will send a discomfort signal if there is backed-up pressure. I'm forced to take time out and transmute it, or it will go from bad to worse.

"That's weird."

"Yes, I know. When I got to this ring, I felt it in my head."

"My body talks to me, too, when something comes through," Abe said, "but I don't always feel it in the same spot."

"Well, I guess I'm a bit strange, but I'm okay with it, now."

"Did you experience any of your inner demons? On either one of these first layers?"

"Yes, some fears came up that I thought I had worked through. One was a recurring dream of being chased. It came from a trauma I experienced as a child when I fell out of a tree and hurt myself. I fell following an elemental spirit up a tree, but I didn't understand at the time that I could fall."

"How old were you?"

"Oh, five, I think. I don't know why, but ever since then, I have had this dream. I think I have faced it now. This time, I turned around and looked that fear square in the face. I felt a release that I hadn't been able to reach before. There is something about being here that helped me face it this time.

"There's a magic to this mountain."

"Yes, there is, but you haven't seen anything yet."

Ty nodded. "I fear for someone who's clueless about energy if they try to come up this mountain."

"That's for sure. I can see why someone might think they were going crazy if they came under this energy dome," he said with a throaty chuckle. "It would be really scary for them."

Ty asked him what he experienced when he first came to the woods. "How did you react?

No one warned you, right?"

"Right, but my mother told me a little bit about it. It really started when I walked through the old stone entrance by the waterfall. Later, when I went back to check on the energy there, my intuition told me it represented our heart's multidimensional gateway."

"That's an interesting name for it."

"Yes, it is."

"I interrupted you because I felt a rush of energy around the name."

"Me too. I heard a strong, authoritative voice tell me he was the gatekeeper of that entrance. 'The way that leads you home to your source,' he said. When I tuned in, I saw a cone-shaped tunnel of pink light. It reminded me of that weird spider that weaves a wormhole, which looks like a cone. Do you know the one I'm talking about?" Ty asked.

"I don't know its name, but I've seen it — it's awesome." "Well, the one I saw was so beautiful--there are no words to describe it."

"I can only imagine," Abe said. "By the time I reached the woods, I was almost doubled over. I felt sick to my stomach. At first, I wondered if I had eaten something that had gone bad. I threw up, and afterward, these voices started chattering nonstop in my head. I finally realized that my fears had been triggered by that place. I guess my egos remembered all the stories we've heard that this forest was haunted." He chuckled.

"What's tickling you?" she asked shyly. "If you aren't comfortable talking about it, that's okay." She was surprised at herself for asking him such a personal question.

"Oh, no, it's okay." He was still chuckling. "When I was younger and stupid, I was with my friend Lance and another kid, Joe. They played a joke on me. You see, I had boasted about not being afraid of anything, so they decided to put me to the test. It was sometime later when they asked me if I would go on a hunting trip with them. I had forgotten about my brag. I reluctantly agreed to go. I never liked killing anything, but I decided to go, anyway. On the first night, we started hearing noises while we sat around the campfire. Lance was clearly getting scared, or so I thought, and Joe kept making it worse. They put on a good show for me, and I got scared, too. They had a mutual friend in the woods, making all these sounds as if the woods were haunted. They got me good. When the voices in my head started up, here, I flashed back to that experience. I thought I had cleared it, but I guess I hadn't. Your head will say one thing, and your emotions another. I sure had a charge left around it, I found out."

Ty giggled.

"Like you said earlier, I had to be willing to investigate the reflection mirrored in that old trauma. I learned that my genetics still had some unresolved issues that were hidden from me. They all hit me in the face, and I couldn't proceed until I had looked at them. That's why I say the outer rim is about our egos and the false stories we've been telling ourselves. The first and second rings seem to deal with our ego personalities and their link with corresponding emotional patterns. It seems to be a basic principle. You can't have one without the other. One is just more upfront than the other.

"As my brother used to say, it's piggybacked."

"Yes, that's a good way to put it. When I reached the second ring, it was easier because I finally figured it out. I realized multiple shielding rings guarded this place from outsiders. For me, the first and second were the hardest to get through. The rest were more of a breeze after I cleared myself from ancestral ties that had kept me attached to the collective. Even though I was no longer asleep to the internal way of life, I found out that I was still bound by some old genetic habits. I thought I was past all of that, but it wasn't true. My body sure taught me some things about my old, subconscious stuff. The body is a great teacher when you've learned to listen to it."

"Yes, for sure. Which part got the most attention from you?"

Abe continued, "I would have to say my pain body, and my emotions. I've never felt anything like it outside of here. It woke up parts of myself that I didn't know were there. I found I had some old judgment that my body was still holding on to. And, honestly, I've experienced surprisingly new levels of feeling. I know the difference, now, in the voices I hear. I've heard them for most of my life. They always confused me about which one to follow. Early in my teenage years, I learned how to tell the difference by the feeling that came with them. Were they fear-ridden, or not? That helped a lot, but coming here took me deeper and put me in touch with the hidden, antagonist part of myself, the part we saw last night, that part that wants to resist anything that has to do with the mother."

"Oh, I also realized that I gave birth to my female side as never before. I still can't believe that, for my whole short life, I didn't know the difference. I would have sworn I did, but I didn't. It's been a real awakening, especially since last night. I can't get it out of my head. It sure puts a whole new twist on things."

"Yes, for sure."

"I feel so much more complete," he said with deep intensity.

"It sounds like you gave birth to a new feeling body."

"That rings true."

They walked for a while. "There's a rocky area coming up," he warned her.

"Worse than what we've already been through?"

"I wouldn't normally come through here, but it will save us some time. It's also one of the most beautiful spots I've found. You'll love it, and I'll get a real workout. So, I might need to stop a few times to get a breather.

"Okay," she said, but she felt a little concerned.

They came through a band of conifers, which abruptly stopped on the edge of a bluff with an outcropping of big boulders. Beyond that lay a wide expanse. "This is it," Abe said.

"Oh, it's magnificent, but do you think you can get me through that terrain? It's steep and treacherous."

"I know it looks that way, but I found a path. We'll be ok."

"Really?"

"Yes, several days ago, I went that way and even camped there for a night," Abe said.

"Trust me."

"Okay," she said, still a little in doubt.

The descent was no longer a path but a step from rock to rock, weaving in between large boulders. All the while, he had to maintain his balance with her in his arms. There was no room for error. When they safely reached the bottom and he started up to the other side, he quickened his pace. His breathing became heavier and heavier until, finally, he said: "I'm going to need a breather." He found a large, flat rock to set her on. After a brief rest, he picked her up again.

"I don't know how you're able to do this?"

"I grew up climbing mountains. We even had a big cave I used to explore, so don't worry about me." He was still panting loudly. Once they reached the peak, he sat her down again and took a drink. He glanced up at a higher elevation just in time to see several mountain goats scrambling across a rugged outcropping: "Look!" he said, pointing.

"Oh, my," she said. "That's the first I've ever seen! What a sight!"

"Glad we found that creek back there," he said.

Ty sat on the stone for just a few moments before she felt a familiar zing. "Do you feel the energy here?" she asked.

"I don't notice it right now, but when I slept here, I sure did. This seems to be a power spot on the grid here."

"There is something special about this place." She sensed the presence of gnomes around the area. "Do you see the gnomes?" she whispered.

"No, I don't. Are you picking up on them?"

"Yes, there is a whole family here."

He sat down and relaxed his focus. "Wow, there they are!"

"They are telling me they have given you some much-needed strength."

"Yeah, they saw my special cargo."

"That's what they're indicating." Ty's curiosity was aroused by a few who were standing apart from the others. Then she heard that those would be continuing the journey with them. "Really?"

"Yes, we have been waiting for you to come back. There is a great celebration that has been called, and we are following you back for it," one of the gnomes said.

"What is this celebration about?" she asked.

"The entire elemental kingdom is having a party," the husky voice said. "We're to celebrate your return to the mountain.

"Okay," Abe said. "Welcome, we will be happy to have you join us." He picked her up and started their descent, again, through the steep, rocky terrain.

When the land leveled out, she sensed that he was affecting her. She tried to discount it as, perhaps, just imagination. She decided to let it go for the moment. But found herself speaking it out loud: "I am concerned that our heartbeat and breathing seem to be affecting me."

"I'm not surprised. Our fields have been enmeshed while I've been carrying you," Abe said. Suddenly, he was caught off guard for a moment and stumbled. Her eyes flew open. He looked down at her:

"Sorry for disturbing you."

"Oh, I'm fine. I wasn't asleep."

He tried to explain that he was a little out of breath and that he almost tripped over a rock.

He shifted his hold around her body and steadied himself.

"I am feeling a little guilty about being carried," Ty said.

"Breathe and let it go," Abe said. "I'm fine. I just need to take it slow and carefully."

She turned back to watch him maneuver around the boulders and trees on the trail. "Look at the beauty surrounding us in this part of the forest. The aspens seem like guardians for us," Ty said.

They were climbing again. She marveled at his strength and endurance, his stamina. He was in excellent shape. She wondered how much help he was getting from their invisible taga-longs. She decided to check on them. No one was behind them, but when she checked up ahead, there they were, the whole clan. Several small children, she assumed, were going into a boulder and jumping out the other side.

"What?" he asked. She looked up with a puzzled look on her face. "I saw you open your eyes, and then you smiled."

"Oh, that. I was smiling at the gnomes. The little ones were having a lot of fun."

"I remember seeing something like that once," he grinned.

When they finally reached a flatter terrain and he started breathing a little easier, he looked down at her: "Wow, I'm getting a workout!"

"Yes, I've noticed," she smiled.

"I chose this way because I knew it was faster, but I hadn't thought it through about carrying someone. "Don't get me wrong," he added quickly before she could say anything. "Don't go into guilt. I love this jaunt, and I love having you in my arms."

"You sure?"

"Very sure, madam. I love this sort of thing. I live for it, my mother used to say. It's a good exercise to boot." He smiled down into her eyes.

The path had gotten a lot smoother, so he could walk with greater ease. The woods were quiet except for an occasional crow. "I've been thinking about our earlier conversation," he said.

"Which one?"

"The one when we were talking about going through the Rings of Light together."

"Oh, yeah. It's so new to me. I don't know what to say, and last night's experience makes it even harder."

"Yes, I know. I've been going over what I experienced the first time and comparing it to this time with you. This is completely different than before. It must be important that we do this together to merge our proxies better before the others come. That's a little vague, but do you know what I'm saying?"

"Yes, welcome to my reality."

He laughed: "What do you mean?"

"My whole life has been that way. I don't always get the overview like you've explained.

It's nice to finally get some help."

"What help?"

"You told me how to get through the Rings of Light."

"Oh, yes, sure."

"Well, that was a big help. I don't think it's all about us getting there faster. I agree with you: it feels important that it happened this way. I know that we'll understand it more later. I'll have a dream that kind of shows me something, but then I still must walk it out before I understand what it's all about. My point is that I don't always have a conscious overview that I can sink my teeth into, like your earlier explanation. My guidance gives me some direction, then I must walk it out in blind faith and trust. Afterward, I'll understand it a lot better. The process has helped me to build a strong sense of confidence and trust in my guidance, but it helps to receive some steps laid out ahead of time for a change."

"Okay, I guess I need to archive that," Abe said. "When you follow guidance, you don't always know what it's about.

"I think I've had a judgment around it," she said with a sense of realization in her voice. "That's a great insight." She was silent for a few moments as she processed this new understanding. "I need to let it go. We can develop a new perception, an ability to know something ahead of time. That's one of the things we're doing. We're developing this as we work together here."

"Wow, this is amazing," he chuckled. "Well, Madam, I'm glad I can help," he bowed slightly. "I guess I just haven't had much time to integrate all that's happening, especially in walking it out, like you're saying. That's it!" He looked surprised. "Inspiration only becomes a part of your life after you've applied it.

"Yes, you might perceive something spiritually, but until you start to apply it — give it expression in some activity — it can't be fully realized or understood. It's a universal principle. We can easily overlook this because we become captivated by our ability to think," she concluded.

"You're right. We need to be aware of this so that we can understand how to manifest things in our lives. And, I have to admit, I pay more attention to my ideas than to ways of giving them expression in my life. My mother knew this, but I haven't consciously practiced it like you have. I guess that's an area I need to work on. You've helped to clarify this for me."

"Well, that's why I say we needed to do what we did last night. We needed to help repair our culture's lack of understanding."

"Yes. Now, I want to re-dream my first experience when I came through here. I'll do it while I'm taking you through the circles!

"Perfect!"

"Okay, I need to finish what I was saying earlier." He gave her a quick glance. "I'm sure that you already know most of this, so it's probably redundant. I don't want to bore you."

"I won't be, I'm sure. We both need to understand each other better. How I would explain something is always going to be different than you, and vice versa. And it's always good to learn from another person, to see the ancient teachings from their point of view. For me, it's interesting to hear how the story of our origins has been passed down through the different clans. Just act like I'm a newbie who doesn't know any of this. But truthfully, I live for this kind of stuff, so go ahead."

"Oh, okay," he shrugged. "I just wanted to get that out of the way. I like to see things through a new set of eyes, too. There are some other perspectives I need to share with you." He was silent while internally he searched his thoughts for what he needed to cover and how to communicate it. A feeling emerged in response to that question and, with it, a clear sense of how to proceed. "Here, within the energy bands, the current physical body must get free of the foreign genetics that have hijacked the body. In going through the first two rings, you begin to detach yourself from the collective consciousness and the grid that it has created. According to my understanding, these changes were made possible by our original separation from Source. We have accepted a system of beliefs from the collective, but we can choose to let go of these limitations. They must be recycled and mutated. It's then that you start to become an individual, a self who is no longer part of a hive-minded type of collective. That is a trap that we fell into in the past. We have the possibility of exchanging our old, outdated grid for a revised one once we reconnect with our true source."

"The central energy dome represents the new divine grid that supports the inner changes we're going through. By intentionally going through the outer gateway, we choose to go through the steps of initiation, to die to the old, collective beliefs to be reborn onto a new grid that supports an inner, divine life. This exchange allows physical and spiritual genetics to co-exist on the same plane. As we progress through each ring, a circuit is re-established between us and the Source of our omnipresent mind. We are reverse engineering ourselves. When we reach the fifth layer through this exercise, we have found our true energetic core, our universal essence of life, light, and love, the three L's my mother called them."

"Multidimensionally, we have re-grounded ourselves in Mother Earth's loving embrace as a unified bio-field. This weaves our soul with the soul of Gaia. Prior to this, a major component of our lives was missing. Overall, Zathera represents a field that holds this connection for the whole planet."

"I've seen it like an anchor. It's a doorway into the higher realms of the infinite mind that we were separated from long ago. I don't know how all that works, yet, but I know one thing: this place will reveal many mysteries that we would never be able to comprehend outside of here. I do promise you that," he said emphatically. "Do you get the gist of what I'm saying?"

"Yes, I think I do." She closed her eyes to breathe in all he had said. "I've got to remember this and hold these keys close. I'm saving what I have just heard, as part of my overall editing program. That's how I learn to apply new information. If it doesn't feel right, I delete it." Ty paused for a moment. "This makes me happy. I feel it all aligning nicely. Nothing is at war in me."

"I like what you just did," he commented.

"It's taken some time to put it into practice and make it a beneficial habit."

"How do you mean?"

"You know how hard it is to get out of the head."

"Oh, yeah."

"I've learned to watch my thoughts, catch any negative ones, and then reprocess them. Most of the time, I decree that this is not the reality I align with anymore, and then I neutralize the negative charge with a spinning vortex of unconditional energy. Technically, I flood any harmful energy with divine love to transform it. I place myself on my heart's throne to determine whether something is in balance. Above all, I'm searching for any warring energy."

"Wow, I'll have to adopt that process."

"I've found it to be quite helpful."

"I like how it feels," he added.

8. The Fourth Ring

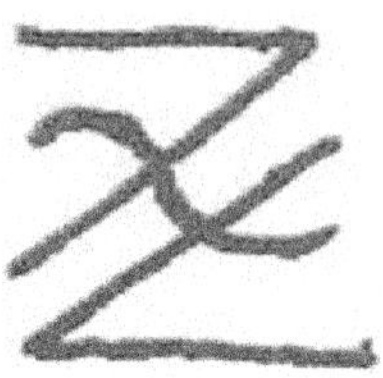

"Okay, back on track. Where was I regarding the four Rings? Do you feel you have enough information about these levels?" he asked her.

"Okay, so the third has to do with the emotional or pain body, right?"

"Yes, I guess you could say that."

"Then I think I have a good sense of what it represents. I'll be dealing with any residual emotional issues I haven't faced yet."

"Yes."

"Hmm. I don't have a clear picture around the fourth, yet. Please remind me."

"Okay, on the fourth, you must drop your old limiting beliefs around the current physical body, such as shame, judgments, death, and dying. It also includes all our programmed beliefs that we picked up from the ancestral mythologies of our gods and that whole hierarchical system."

"Originally, the body was never meant to die; it was your decision when to lay it down. We have been programmed to believe in death. That, too, must be released. Our body's genetics carry around all this junk. Dropping all of it will lift the weight off the physical body. It needs to be loved rather than judged and used like a packhorse. Its legacy is not to carry the crap of collective consciousness. It wasn't born out of sin. That's a lie. The body needs to be accepted and respected, not lorded over. All of this must be resolved. The body is wanting, no, demanding it, we must recognize its importance and love it to live. In many ways, there seems to be more here than on the other layers. I've learned that the body is holding a lot of resentment."

"Oh, I almost forgot this experience," he added. "I felt as if my body slapped me in the face. It took some time to figure out. It was so strong that I had to tune in to get more understanding. The door to my genetics had been sealed to keep me out, but by asking the right question, I could get in. It's weird how it works. After what we went through last night, I have a new perspective. I needed to understand this for all my brothers so that we can realize that we have a right to change our current programming if we want to. Each of us can heal the split in our being, just like females have to do in their own way. We can open to being unconditional and drop our judgmental, harsh, unloving attitudes concerning our bodies and women. For me, I would have to say I learned the most about myself on this layer."

Abe continued, "I see now that when I walk you through the fourth realm, I'm going to add a few more aspects around what happened last night. We must change this split inside of us forever. I don't want to have a battle going on inside of me; I want to repair what's been broken in my genetics. I want to have a new relationship with a woman that goes way beyond just a sexual relationship to reproduce and have a family. I want a loving, respectful kind of relationship. I want to be whole inside me, first and secondly, have a partner who has also healed their state of separation. I choose to know what that kind of divine relationship would be like. In partnering up with an equal, you learn much faster because you're on the same journey of self-discovery. I hear it's a lot more fun when you do it with a partner," he said as he looked at her and smiled. "I want to develop my feminine half alongside a woman who embodies it. This way, we can help each other grow. I feel I've done this in past lifetimes, and now, I want to build on that relationship we once shared together. I know I have prepared my whole life for what is unfolding here at Zathera. I don't understand it all yet, but I'm learning to stay open and trust the process as I walk it out. See. I'm learning fast, right?"

"Yes, you are."

***

She could see his heart. She could read between the lines and see it through his words. He was being totally honest with her. She noticed him shifting himself as she looked deeper into his soul. She sensed some inner aspect had come forward and had been partially speaking through him. The rest he knew from his own experience. His true nature was revealing itself.

"Whoa! That was deep," he exclaimed. "It's been hard to stay rooted and grounded ever since I went through my initiations. I assume I'm still in transition."

"Yes, I would agree. I saw your heart speaking. I can see you have healed your split. It was beautiful to watch." She quickly glimpsed into what their future was going to look like. He was the perfect outer example, one who reflected her inner divine nature. He would be wonderful to partner with on their Earth Walk. While they were in this embodiment, they would walk that path side-by-side. In their tradition, they didn't need someone to feel complete, but it was about choosing to grow and learn faster by having a partner. For them, it was about finding a partner who was your equal so that you could have a balanced relationship. That was why they called their mate a partner rather than a husband or a wife, terms that had more of a possessive quality. They were trying to shift that old paradigm of thinking that the male had to dominate his wife. Their union might also reflect issues connected to still unresolved karma or genetic lessons. They called this 'soul reflections.' It also occurred to her that their two overlapping fields created their She'sta body. Their children would come through this unified body consciousness.

She knew all too well how their genetics still carried many pitfalls. By partnering up with a sacred soul who was on the same divine journey, they would become teachers, students, and healers for each other. A divine partner who reflects any unresolved issues can speed up the process of healing tremendously. This was what they would agree to if they decided to merge as divine partners. This kind of relationship would be the ultimate reflective therapy. Together, they would have a companionship known as a divine coupling. *Oh, I am going to love this divine specimen,* she thought to herself. *He will be my beloved.* She would see him as an outer reflection of her inner male. That would be her focus. He would outwardly assist her in continuing to rebuild her bridge to her divine, androgynous nature which still existed but on the other side. It was her intent in life to heal this separation within herself. Abe broke into her thoughts and pulled her back to finish his explanation. Right now, he was being her teacher, and she welcomed it.

***

"Okay, I'm back," she said as she locked on to his every word.

"By the time you reach the fifth Ring or dome, you are energetically beyond the realm of third density that evolved out of

138

separation. You've re-attuned yourself to your original body consciousness, created as an offspring of the omnipresent mind. You've spiritually shifted paradigms because you returned to your body's original template, which is beyond time: no more past, present, or future. You are in the now moment. As you know, this is different than how most people understand it. They think they are stepping upward and out of the body in vibration, out of the third dimension, and into the fifth. However, we're talking about a totally different direction to the ascension process. I like the word transformation. They are energetically trying to go upward and outward. They don't realize they are following the direction they were encoded with because they are trying to get out of this body that they have judged so heavily."

Abe paused for a moment. "We dive and go inward because we see that the body can be multi-dimensional, limitless, and universal in nature. Everything is inside of this beloved body. This is taking your body with you, not leaving it behind. Our path is to go inward into the quantum core and touch our source power. Walking inwardly takes you into an altered frequency, beyond time. This takes you beyond the range of the E.T. dynamics. These two different paths need to be understood so that you know what you are aligning yourself to, either the old system designed to keep us under control or our inner legacy from the beginning, by which we are connected to our source and on the path to becoming a self."

"I know this is confusing to some, but it needs to be understood so you can make an informed decision. This is what we're revising so that the physical body can remember the life it once knew when it was free of pain and suffering, as we know it now. This inner process reactivates a core life gene that is now dormant. It recodes our current physical genetics for us to wake up and remember how to live life with joy. Here you become your own inner authority, one with your source."

Ty looked puzzled. "I'm sorry, am I going too fast?" Abe asked.

"No," Ty replied. "It's a lot to take in. I'm trying to assimilate your perceptions, that's all. I get it."

"Okay, back to the Fifth. The frequency at this level carries you into a spiritual dimension that is technically universal in nature, beyond this physical realm. You have stepped out of the planetary sphere of duality and into an inner world. You now live between the folds of space and time, rather than in time and space. That's a brain twister, isn't it?" He glanced at her to see how she was taking it.

"Yes, but I understand what you're saying."

"Great," he said as he refocused on his steps again. "You've walked out of that old life. You've broken free of the chains around your physical body. Fear and limitation are gone. You've dropped the body's shroud; you've transcended the tree of knowledge of good and evil.

"Once you stand before the old arched gateway at the entrance of Zathera, you will have completed the energetic journey home. You will have emerged from a wormhole that penetrated the dimensional depths of your heart to your very core. Inside that space, we have yet to learn what life will be like." Abe stopped and looked at her, making sure she understood him. He saw no hint of confusion in her face, so he continued, "I saw myself inside of this glowing tunnel woven of threads of every color of the rainbow. The entrance to the tunnel started at the old collapsed stone circle near the waterfall, and it went through all of the dimensional rings of light, ending at the gate of Zathera. It was breathtaking!" He momentarily became caught up in remembering his experience that first time. "Wow! That was a process to put into words," he said when he finally snapped out of it.

"I'll bet," she said with a smile.

"You understand what I've said, right?"

"Yes, I think so … or I should say I feel that I do. It's a lot to process. Thanks for your insights." She paused for a moment. "When you reach the center of Zathera, you are energetically out of this dimension, out of this world, did I understand you correctly?"

"Yes, that's what I understand. You've become a universal divine soul."

"Gee, you've given me a lot to think about."

***

They walked on in silence for quite some time while she thought about what he had said. She felt she had a good sense of each of the energy bands she was experiencing and felt lucky to have his feedback about his experience. It was easy to see why it was important for them to do this together. He had to be the first for him to consciously pave the way for her and anyone else who might return. She didn't fully understand everything, but she could sure feel the energy behind it.

"Do you think that we're going to get there before dark?" she asked.

"Well," he said between heavy breaths, "we've been doing good. We should make it if we keep pushing, and if I can physically hold up while you make the shifts at each new band. We'll see how it goes. I know these woods now, and I have learned some shortcuts, so I think we can make it."

They passed the time by playing games in between working with the transition zones.

One was to acknowledge all the different, mammoth tree species they saw.

"They are ancient tree beings," she told Abe. Once, Ty thought she saw a tree that was pulling its roots out of the earth to follow them. She filed it away and invited them to come if they could. Next, they moved to the smaller plant species. They selected different plants in their line of vision to see if they could identify them. If they recognized one, they would share the information they knew about it. He was surprised at how well she knew most of the common so-called weeds, herbs, and flowers.

"See, I told you I wasn't as familiar with the herbal kingdom as you are," he said.

"You knew many of them, though," replied Ty.

"But you knew way more than I did."

***

After a while, he got tired of the game and changed the subject:

"What do you think of the haunted forest, now?"

"Oh, it's very scary," she teased. "You better not go in there."

"No? Why?" He burst into laughter. "I've loved every moment of being here. I've spent weeks now scouting the east and south range of this mysterious place. I love to explore, so I've had a blast. This range is so beautiful. I've never seen anything like it! It's magical. The size of the trees at Zathera will astound you. The closer we get to the core, the bigger they grow. I just know it has to do with this place and the relationship our ancestors had with it.

You'll see what I'm talking about when we get there. They must have lived in perfect harmony with this place because everything here loves humans. I won't say anything else about it right now because you won't believe me until you see it yourself."

"All I can say is, on this mountain, the nature spirits still exist here openly. To me, it indicates that this place lives between the folds of space and time. One of the most beautiful places here, besides the waterfall below, is a place not too far from the village. It's the actual headwaters that feed this whole mountain. The area around the spring is breathtaking. The water that comes up out of the earth carries the essence of pure life. It nourishes everything in a way I've never experienced before. The essence of the Spirit that infuses these sacred waters is very healing. I can't wait to swim in it again. Whenever you get to feeling better, I'll take you. I'm sure it'll speed up your healing process. What am I saying? If I am carrying you now, then I can take you there, too! Tomorrow, I'll take you, if you want?"

"Of course."

"Drinking the water is healing, too. I watched my energy change every day as I drank the water. It aligns me with my core energy and makes me feel in harmony with everything around me. You know, I used to think my body was doing great, but after being here for a while, I found that wasn't true. Yes, I was doing as well as I could, but this space gives a boost to the whole transformational process. Those who created it loved and respected the earth; they must have shared a remarkable relationship with Gaia's spirit."

He paused. "There's something else that's mysterious about Zathera. One evening, I walked out to the garden. There aren't as many trees there, so I could see more of the night sky. The moon had just come up—it was full—as big as I'd ever seen it. Then, I saw something else."

"What?" she asked eagerly.

"At first, I thought there was a halo around the moon, but when I looked closer, I saw it to be a golden dome of energy over this whole mountain." It seems to be an invisible shield over Zathera to protect it from the outside world. It's a beautiful sight to see, but it can only be seen during the rays of the full moon." He looked over at her, expecting her to say something, but her mind seemed to have gone somewhere, so he concentrated on walking carefully.

"I just saw the field of energy within the Golden Dome and all the layers within it. I guess they were the rings that surrounded each initiation step. I saw the five-layered fields of this dome that you talked about. There's a massive geometrical-like grid that's the foundation for the rings. I've never seen anything like it! A tube of light in the center supports the entire protective field. It mesmerized me!"

She looked up in his face: "Have you seen it?"

"I guess I have to say yes and no," he confessed. "I see the individual rings, how they interconnect, and how they affect anyone who enters, but I've never experienced the core. I'll have to go on an inner journey to see it for myself."

"Yes, you must, because there is no way I could ever explain what I just saw. Oh, my gosh!" she said. "I feel myself immersed in the energy once more." She paused as if in thought. "I left right after the full moon, so I guess it'll be in a couple of weeks before the next one," she said, reluctantly. "Darn, I'll have to wait." Suddenly, like a little child, her excitement came back: "Oh, it'll be worth the wait! I guess I need to be satisfied that I saw it from inside," she smiled.

He just had to smile. She was so adorable. They walked in silence for a bit, then he continued to explain how the golden energy affected everything that was under it. "Life of every kind thrives under that energy. It is so magical; it must be one of a kind."

"But from what I've heard, there's supposed to be two places like this mystery school," she explained.

"I know," he said, "but I really wonder about that. How can there be another place set up like this? Just wait, and you'll see as we begin to get closer to the center. I am curious. Look what it took to create a place like this. How could there be another one?"

"I guess we may never know, but one thing is for sure, this place is real!"

"My curious side would love to know where it is."

"Yes, me too."

***

She thought about it some more. It all rang true in her. She had already witnessed some of what it had provided. There were berries and plums to eat, the trees were huge, and she hadn't seen any carnivorous animals that wanted to have them for a meal. She had only seen those that eat from the plant kingdom. This place evoked a sense of pure magic and mystical beauty, and she felt its reflection in every cell of her body. She already experienced an amazing healing just by being under the canopy of this energy field. She had seen similar injuries that needed days to heal. Her head was clear. There was no headache of any kind, no dizziness, and she had no problem keeping her focus. Even her leg wasn't experiencing much pain until she put her full weight on it. She had no trouble believing what he was saying.

"We're close to the fourth perimeter," he said, "so you may start feeling some new sensations. I think we've got time to stop for a little while. I could use a break."

"Sounds good," she agreed. "I am so excited to finally get there. Zathera has been in my dreams for as long as I can remember."

He looked down at her. "How do you know you've been dreaming about Zathera?"

"It's more of an inner knowing. It just feels right," she replied.

"I know what you mean. That's how I experience it as well.

"I think it's in our blood."

"Yes, I think you're right."

They had just sat down when a sudden breeze came up, but there was no sign of movement among the tree leaves, which didn't make sense. *Was that just a whirlwind of energy,* she wondered. As he picked her up again, she asked him, "Did you feel that?"

"Oh, that," he said as if it was nothing.

"What do you mean, 'oh that?'"

"Well, it's just something you'll have to get used to while you're here. I felt it, too. Most likely it was some nature spirits. There are times when they like to play and make themselves known. Other times, it's the ancients or the omnipresent guardians that enjoy making themselves known, too. I didn't take the time to tune in because we needed to keep moving. It's getting late. That is one of the reasons I know this place exists between the realms. The veils are so thin here that you can feel many spiritual forms. Just wait. You'll have some of your own experiences to go along with this one," he warned her.

"I can't wait. That will be fun."

She laid her head against his chest and noticed some new sensations moving through her. "I'm picking up on something. Any ideas?"

"Well, I had some strange experiences at this point," he said. "Here is where you start connecting to the real elemental energies that make up Zathera. At this point, you are opening to a new level of spiritual existence because your sensitivities have changed. I had a déjà vu experience. The landscape was identical, I had just returned from a long walk, and I felt exuberantly alive. We are now entering new levels that your body hasn't aligned with before, and from here on, the external plane is behind you. You have released a certain amount of density, and now you're aligning to the central energy tube at the core of the mountain, at the village. You are feeling that old energy drop away, transitioning into the energy forces of the core. That's why you are feeling so weird. Everything that is not the true light of unconditional love is being released. By the time you get to the center, everything will have been swapped over to the divine circuitry."

"How did you feel going through this?" she asked.

"I had to hold my focus. That's not easy. I knew I was forming a new body consciousness, and I had to consciously decree that I had power from my source. This awareness seemed very important. I remember at one point I was shaking and trembling as the old constructs came tumbling down within me and around me. It was a weird feeling."

"Wow, you had quite an experience!"

"Yes, I did," he said. "I decreed that I recognized my inner being."

"Well, that makes complete sense."

"How do you mean?"

"The male side is more strongly connected to the mental body than the female. You know this."

"So, it just makes sense that I had to consciously archive this because the mental body needs to be brought into balance. Our thinking and our egos pull our focus outside. Yes, I see where you are coming from."

"And, secondly, the two of us need to be the forerunners to set up a new imprinting for those that follow," she added.

He began to chuckle. She looked at him with a smile on her face: "What?"

"I just remembered something. My Mother always tried to pound this into my head, too. I admit sometimes I could be stubborn. She would say if your body is breathing, then you are alive, right? Well, not really, she would say. That is a mental belief because you breathe, you're alive. The internal forces must be acknowledged; it's this intelligence that bonds these forces together to sustain the life of the body. It's Life that gives you the ability to find your pot of gold. 'Your heart is the end of the rainbow,' she would always say. 'It's all inside of you, encoded deep in your heart.'" He chuckled again. "When I was young, she would tap my head and then my heart as she'd say, 'This is yours and yours alone. It can't be taken from you. It is all yours. It's your treasure chest, a gift freely given when they created your body for you. This is the true source of life, and when you re-awaken to this understanding, you will have rekindled your dormant life spark. Even though you've been taught this, you'll still have to have your awakening so that you know you have experienced it for yourself. Then nobody can take your truth away from you.'" He chuckled. "She worked hard trying to get it through this noggin. When I went through those few days, I got it. Nobody can ever take my knowing from me. I know what I know, just like she was trying to tell me."

***

Up ahead, he finally saw his marker where the fifth Ring began. He needed to stop and relax his shoulders. He had almost reached his limit for the day. "Do you see that little tree up there with an old log and boulders sitting around it? It's the beginning of the fifth Ring. We'll stop there. Are you sensing anything yet?"

"Oh, yes, I have for a while now. I'm feeling a huge shift in my energy fields and my gut."

He put her down on an old log.

"What would you suggest I do at this point?" she asked.

"All of your outer bodies are going to need to be realigned to this frequency, like I said. That is the most important thing to do. When you go through it, you'll know what to do next. Everybody's experience will be different. After that's done, ask if there might be something else you aren't aware of. Use your guidance; trust it. I don't know what you might need to do since you aren't a male. I sense that it will be different for you than it was for me."

9. *The Lifting of the Veils*

When he felt rested, he looked over at her to evaluate her well-being. She met his glance and smiled: "I'm ready to go relieve myself, and then we can go."

After he had her in his arms again, he asked how she handled the energy.

"It went well," she told him. "Once I had my fields adjusted and realigned, I tuned into what lay before me. At first, I saw a wall that stood between me and my goal. I knew it was my final test to break through the veil of this outer reality, as you had explained. I knew I had chosen to enter this dimensional plane and the density that I had to take on here. Intuitively, I realized I had to choose to leave it all behind. I saw that, after conception, my spirit slipped on this bodysuit, which reflects the separation here. So, I perceived that I had to choose to unzip it and step out of its energetic hold on my physical genetics. I saw all these tentacles being extracted. After that was done, I turned back to look at the wall and watched it slowly disappear as it rippled through my energy shell. Then I asked to see what was next. This time I saw the most beautiful golden band of light. A door appeared in it, and I knew I was ready to enter it.

Did you see anything like that?"

"Yes, sort of. I saw a curtain lift in front of me, and a golden energy streamed through from the other side. It formed a foundation, and, as I moved forward, the golden layer solidified under my feet."

"Whoa! I saw it! Did you see where it lifted?"

"Yes, it was that patch of grass off to the right."

"Well, the door I saw is right up there between those two trees." Abe looked to see where she was pointing. "Up there, by that stone with the point on top, next to the two trees that make a sort of door frame."

"Oh, they do." His face lit up with surprise. "Are you ready to go through it?"

***

"Yes." She took several deep breaths as Abe did the same. Together, they stepped into the veiled kingdom. Tingles moved up and down her body as if something washed over her. "I'm returning home," she thought. The tingles gave way to a flood of warmth. Inside, she heard, *I'm loved unconditionally*. She felt like a newborn being welcomed into the world. Breathing in this new awareness brought up a memory of returning home after a long trip with her uncle years earlier. She was so happy to be back in familiar surroundings. *Yes, that's what I'm feeling. I'm coming home.* Her body remembered. She felt like crying. Tears welled up, and a few slowly slid down her cheeks. She started sniffling.

"Are you ok?" Abe asked.

"Yes, I'm just having this overwhelming feeling of coming home. I'm feeling happy, not sad."

"I know what you mean."

She laid her head against his chest to just relax and take in the moment. Something triggered a reminder of all the elementals that they had seen as they were coming across the mountain. *Where are they?* she thought. "Where are the gnomes? Oh, my!" she exclaimed. It was as if someone had just pulled back a curtain on a new world. Beings of every size, shape, and color played before her in a dazzling ocean of life. Even the air streamed with currents of tiny, living beings. Off to the side stood the gnomes watching them go past. She wanted to look back, but what bathed the air was too breathtaking, as if the whole kingdom hailed her return. What she thought to be an invisible realm now stretched as far as she could see. *Thanks for giving me a glimpse of your world.* She sent a greeting of pink light from her heart to meet them all. "I love you," she hollered as they proceeded on.

***

Solace accompanied Abe's footsteps as he walked over another rocky hill and down into the next valley. "We're not too far away now," he whispered. The shadows were getting longer. "The sun is starting to go down fast so I'm going to take a shortcut." Privately, he wished that there was enough light to go through the official entrance, but for now, they would have to come in the back way. And while he wanted her in his arms as long as possible, the thought of arriving at their new home excited him. He told himself he would be able to properly court her soon enough, and at some point, they would consummate their union. *I can't wait to show her around Zathera*, he thought. He realized that he had now entered a whole new phase in his life. The courtship between them had already begun. He was smitten. He knew that he had found his life partner. It was a long-standing tradition within their culture to only partner up with someone after you knew that you were completely compatible on all levels. Each one had to have a strong sense of their own true identity. They had to have an inner awareness from their source that they were whole in themselves without the need for anyone else to make them feel complete. Then they were ready for a mate. They could marry and join one another sexually. Hormones should never override the divine path. Life choices should never rely on needing another individual. This kept the bloodline strong. He remembered Mother's words: *You are first complete in yourself, and then you are ready to share your life experiences with another. Life will reflect your connection with the source of all that is in unions like this because you've returned to the flow of Life, the mother of everything. Those who shared these sacred teachings knew that this was the ultimate path when deciding to walk their path alongside another.*

Abe felt complete in his abilities. He matured several years in the few short weeks he'd been here. When the time came for the two of them to join, she would accelerate his growth tremendously because they would help each other to learn. He silently chuckled as he ran back over all that had happened in their short acquaintance. It seemed like they had known each other for weeks. They had accomplished a lot since they met, and most of it was on another plane. Now, they would have to find this same companionship on the external plane. Could they fully bond there, he wondered? They would have to see. He continued to walk at a faster pace.

Two paths circled the back way into the old village and to the back door of his cabin. The proper way to enter the dome was through the center, but he wasn't sure if she could wait until morning. Since it was so late, he quickly checked with his guidance on this plan and received an okay to delay her final initiation rites until the morning. Their whole experience so far had involved breaking the old patterns. She needed help all along the way to reach the center, so this must be okay, he decided. The assistance she received must prove important for some reason. He didn't understand why yet, but he resolved that he would at some point. The prospect of their life together excited him in ways he had never known. He chose a nice and cozy dwelling. It would work well for them, and he had plenty of time to fix something to eat before it got too dark.

I could use some light, he thought. *I wish I had some candles.* He had a plan. Ty would sleep in the bed, and he would sleep on the floor. Tomorrow, he would clean up the other room and refill the old mattress. He hoped they would soon share the same bed. *But I'm not going to rush it. She needed time to completely heal.*

In the meantime, they would get to know each other better. Tomorrow, he would carry her to the healing springs. That's the best medicine for her body. Afterward, they could enjoy lazing around in the sun and take it easy until she healed.

They reached the beautiful, open field on the outskirts of the village. A rolling stream of water meandered through the valley, complete with a rustic, arched bridge. Behind it stood a magnificent circle of ancient, towering stones. The sun setting to their right cast long shadows as if directing their attention to the circle of brightly illuminated giants. *Oh, wow,* he said to himself, *this is astounding*! He had never seen it like this.

He momentarily glimpsed the energy from a multitude of beings that created this beautiful picture for him. Faries of all kinds filled the air around them as if they had come to welcome them back. He had not witnessed this before. He wondered if they had all gathered here to meet them. *What amazing variety! The whole kingdom turned out to witness our return.* The circle stood in the distance like a work of art, painted as only nature could. He wished he had the gift to draw what he saw. Several of the guardians put on a show for them. He started to wake her, but his intuition told him to let her rest. Reluctantly, he walked on through the magical valley. Each step began to feel lighter than the one before. The welcoming party invigorated him. Each step took them closer to the core of the energy dome shielding this mountain. *Thanks, my friends. You are my love. I love who you are inwardly and outwardly. Thank you for your welcome. Guide us home and always be with us.*

He looked down at his cargo again and wished she could also witness what he experienced. He wondered why he hadn't investigated the energy here before. *Was I blocking something? Or maybe it just wasn't time.* Walking through the tall grass towards the bridge, he noticed a strange sensation creeping up his legs, especially the left one. He saw the familiar light-blue grid lines that spread throughout the valley. He smiled to himself and vowed to come back to the circle and spend more time here. He felt the energy dome with its corresponding grid, but it differed now. *Why,* he wondered. *Oh, it's her,* he sensed.

Something new is activating on the grid, he heard. Or perhaps reactivating? *It's been dormant for a long time, but the nature spirits are awakening. Interesting.* He resolved to tune in to it at some point to learn more about it. *Maybe before I go to sleep,* he thought. As he skirted around the stones, he acknowledged the main guardian of the circle and promised to return. He loved the visual effects that the great standing stones created at this time of the evening. The shadows they cast mesmerized him. He stopped for a few moments, taking it all in. Each massive stone towered over his head. Each presented a unique shape and personality. He stood in awe of their ancient presence as he sensed the altar that marked its center. His ancestors built one back home, but nothing like the scale of this circle.

Once they reached the edge of the stones, Ty opened her eyes. "Are we about there?"

"Yes, just beyond those trees over there," he indicated with his head. "That's where the dwelling is."

She saw the towering stones. "Oh, my!" she said in a surprised tone. Her voice turned to a whisper. "That's what I saw!" She almost jumped out of his arms.

"Hold on there, girl!" he said as she wiggled in his arms. "You're going to throw me off balance if you aren't careful."

"Sorry," she said, relaxing. He laughed and she playfully hit him. "I can't help it I'm so excited. I just want to go in there."

"I know," he told her with the gentlest of smiles. "I understand, but it's not yet time. We will, I promise you."

"Just think about how our ancestors used to live here," she murmured. "I've dreamt about coming here my whole life. It's like this place is a part of my soul. Sometimes I remember living here, too, maybe in a past life. I can't explain it. That's just the way it feels."

"I understand. It's the same for me."

She teased him playfully: "No, not you, too?"

"Yes, I have," he smiled back at her. "I've had my own unexplained experiences with this place."

"So, we both have a history here. Together," she said seriously. "Wow."

As they cleared the trees, she saw the back sides of several smaller buildings.

"This is the back way in," Abe said. "Tomorrow, I'll take you around to the entrance so that you can experience it properly." He ducked under several low limbs as they skirted through the underbrush. They went through another, smaller clearing with a stream beyond it. She wanted to stand in the cool water. "Tomorrow," he told her. "We don't have enough time right now."

"It's a delightful spot," she murmured.

"You'll enjoy seeing how the streams run through the whole village. Tomorrow, we will go swimming at the healing springs. It will be good for you. And for my aching back," he groaned with a grin.

Ty frowned. She started to say something when he stopped her. "No, really, I'm fine, I didn't mean my back hurts badly right now. I'm just having fun with you. Sure, I'm getting a workout, but I'm fine, really," he assured her. "I'm just saying how my body will enjoy the water, too."

"You sure?"

"Yes, I'm great. Plus, there are some benefits to carrying a beautiful lady in my arms," he said with a big smile. He stopped, looking down into her startled eyes. Abe realized he caught her off guard with that comment. Before she responded, he leaned over and gently kissed her. They shared the moist softness until he pulled back. They stared into each other's eyes for what felt like an eternity. He finally gave her one last kiss, then straightened up and resumed walking.

"You beat me," Ty said. "I was ready to kiss you!

"What?" he said as he kept his eyes on the darkened, wooded trail.

"Earlier, I resolved not to let another opportunity pass me by," she whispered.

"Really?" he said as he stole a quick glance at her face.

"Yes." She smiled.

"Sorry," he told her, "I need to keep an eye on the trail. Rabbits love to come out at this time of the evening. I don't mean to ignore you. It's getting dark here, and any moment a small critter might dart out and throw me off balance." He walked up to the back of an old cabin. "This is where I'm staying."

"Why?" she asked as they made their way to the back door.

"Because it's small and cozy, and it didn't seem as overwhelming as the big hall. I stayed there for the first few days. Once I looked around and explored, I found this one, and it felt right, perfect, and I didn't need a bigger place then."

"Wow, it still looks in pretty good condition," she said.

"See, I warned you. There are some strange things about this place." He set her down on one leg. "The door sticks badly, so we'll have to walk in." She steadied herself as he took the handle and pushed with his full strength. Even then, it opened reluctantly. He put his arm around her waist and led her through a storeroom and into a darkened room. He hurried back for the backpacks and laid them on the table. A grand old stone hearth plus a couple of countertops with some open shelves filled most of the other side of the room.

"I love the stonework around the hearth," Ty said. "It's so meticulous, like a work of art. It's amazing what a good stone mason can do. My uncle and father taught me how to recognize a master's handiwork when it came to stones. The layout of the cabin seems perfect. Very cozy."

The dining area opened into a spacious living area. The hearth warmed the whole cabin. Abe guided her to a beautifully carved, rustic chair that sat to one side of the fireplace. Before she sat down, she limped across the floor. "Hold on, girl, slow down before you hurt yourself."

"I'm fine. I just want to see what everything looks like before it gets any darker." She went to the front door and tried to pull it open.

"Let me help, Miss Independent. This door sticks, too." He worked on the stubborn door until it finally opened. She walked out onto a spacious porch, but Abe stopped her with his hand and told her to slow down again. "I will get you something to sit on so you can enjoy the view, okay?"

"Sure, okay," as she stood looking around.

He reached for a small stool close by and placed it where she could look out over the old village. "I'm going to start the fire and make something to eat while you soak it all in."

"Sounds good."

"When you're ready to come back in, call me and I'll help," he said with a playful sternness. "And I do mean it."

***

"I hear you," she said, smiling back. She turned to what lay before her. Huge canopies of trees made a wonderful and welcoming setting. As she took it all in, she felt a calmness wash over her. *I have been waiting for this my whole life,* she thought. *To know that I'm finally home.* A few tears welled up in her eyes, and she breathed the feeling through her body. She turned to look at the park with the babbling stream meandering through it. Off to the right sat several other buildings barely discernible in the growing dusk. One looked like the entrance Abe had described. She studied the whole setting that she could see. In the fading light, she barely made out the flowers around the cabins that circled through the village. All of the buildings sat nestled under the massive, overshadowing trees. A true sense of peace and calm flooded over her. *Everything lived in harmony with nature here.*

Several arched bridges added to the magical setting. She drank it all in like the nectar of life. She closed her eyes to experience the place through her other senses. Nature played a symphony for her. She heard the rolling waters tumbling over the stones. Another section of the orchestra joined in, the last few evening notes from a pair of doves overhead. *Wow, this is amazing*. Birds chirped and sang all along the way, but here she felt something entirely new. *Under the canopy of this dome center, their songs have a magical quality.* She felt suspended between time and space in a realm that didn't seem quite so dense. She breathed in this knowledge, like an evening dew that settled into her soul. She rested in its healing balm.

A road surrounded the outer circle of the village with the river feeding each dwelling the water they needed. *Simply amazing.* "Someone went to a lot of trouble to intentionally design all this," she yelled to Abe. "Or maybe nature created this for them, and they enhanced what nature accomplished. This is a prime example of what it could look like if you lived in harmony with nature."

She studied the design of the nearby buildings. She realized that Abe stood in the doorway behind her. "Have you ever seen buildings built like this before?" she asked.

"No, I haven't. but I love the design. They feel so free flowing. It's a weird way to say it but the roofs have the feel of a flowing stream, less constraining and boxy than the houses back home."

"I like how it makes me feel," she told him. "They're unique, and all of the curves change the old building model I'm used to."

"I know what you mean. The curve and the upward tilt of the roofline create that aesthetic."

"And the shutters over the windows, too," she replied. "The accents make it seem otherworldly. I guess it's the whole design that creates that feeling. I like how the roofs have such a huge overhang, and the porches add even more to the design."

"Yes. When it rains, everything underneath is protected."

"How interesting," she thought. She tried, again, to take in the whole village from where she sat. "Are all of the smaller dwellings like this one?"

"Yes. There are a few that are more crudely built but they seem more like a workspace rather than living quarters."

"Why are the buildings in such great condition? As old as they are, they should look dilapidated. They've been abandoned and unattended for how many thousands of years?"

He chuckled out loud seeing the expression on her face.

"Now I think you can see what I meant, right?"

"Yes, I guess so."

"There are many mysteries here that I haven't figured out yet. You just wait. There will be even more."

"Okay, that satisfies my curiosity for now," she said as she turned to him. "I'm ready to go back inside. You do know I'm looking forward to exploring tomorrow, right?"

"Oh, yeah, me too. But right now, you're not going anywhere. Tomorrow we will see how you feel. You're going to need a lot of rest over the next few days. You can relax now that we're here. Nothing is going anywhere; I promise you that."

"Okay, okay," she reluctantly agreed.

"Just think what it would be like if we hadn't made it here tonight. We would be camping along the trail for another day. So be happy you're here," he told her sternly.

"Okay, I'm satisfied to just go to the headwaters. That should be an amazing experience."

"I have the food almost ready," he said as he helped her to a big, oversized chair by the table. "I've made a soup for us."

"Sounds good." She sat back in the grand, old chair and thought about what he told her. As she sat there, she ran her fingers over the beautiful wooden arms. She slowly realized her fingers sank into the surface as if made of thick honey. "Hmm," she said and let herself drift into the sensation. The energy lulled her into a groggy state, and she drifted off. She was startled awake by the sound of Abe stirring an old cast iron pot over the fire.

10. The Healing Chair

"What?" she said.

"You're back."

"I must have dozed off."

"You did."

She remembered caressing the arms of the chair. "There's something about this chair." She closed her eyes to tune into its energy deeper this time. Something responded to her loving caresses. Her uncle, a master craftsman, taught her how to read the energy of wood. He instilled it with a certain energy, and it was her job to pick up on what he embedded in it. "When you enjoy what you create, you imbue a part of yourself into it," he often said. "Infusing something means you give it a new form of life, and you enhance its natural energy with your own. You can do this because of your love and connection with the 'All That Is,'" he explained. "When you are one with all life, you extend and expand on its natural essence." She still recalled the dulcet tone of his voice. "Respect nature first, and you become its medium."

"Let's use a tree, for instance," he would say. "You think it's dead because it was cut down. However, it depends on the belief of the craftsman who finds the wood. If he isn't aware and doesn't know how to tune into it, then it will be dead. But if a true craftsman loves it, then he becomes a medium for life. He can extend its life essence into the new form it's been given, especially if he sets his intention while the tree still stands. If he doesn't know how to do this, then the tree can die forever. Even a log from a fallen tree can be gifted into a new life form," he would add. "It's all about your perception, your belief," he told her. "If you know your connection with all Life, then it lives on because you loved it and gave it another expression in which to experience itself."

A divine craftsman infused this wood with some creative power. She felt it calling her inward, like a sense of it waking up from a long, deep sleep. She became aware that someone loved it to life. It provided her with some needed healing.

"Greetings," a groggy voice spoke.

"Greetings back at you," she told the sleepy, old tree spirit. *No wonder I went to sleep so fast. The chair's spirit was also asleep. Whoever created this chair designed it to heal and restore a tired body.* "Oh, I'll be sitting on you a lot over the next several days," she informed it.

"I am at your service. I am delighted that you understand and feel my gift. I sense you need it, dear one," the tree spirit in the chair said.

"Well, I am honored that you will help me."

He sounded old and gruff, but at the same time, loving and comforting. "I am glad you awakened me," the voice came back. "Thank you."

She opened her eyes and told Abe what she had experienced.

"Wow," he said. He sounded deeply affected and took some time to speak. "You have just answered a life-long riddle. In one respect, I'm on a quest because I've had this recurring vision trying to tell me something, but I haven't been able to understand what it meant. The visions never made any sense."

"What's wrong?"

"Oh, nothing's wrong. My family never had this legacy around wood crafting like yours. That's why I've been so mesmerized by the trees here. I know they are part of my answer because my visions always center around mammoth trees and their spirit. They try to talk to me, but I can't interpret what's being said, and I wake up frustrated."

She began to get up. "What are you doing?" he asked.

"You must come over here and check it out for yourself."

"I have already, but I had no inkling of what you experienced."

"All I can say is it takes some practice to connect with its spirit. You need to consciously connect with the spirit of the wood.

"Okay," he said as he walked over to the chair, paused, and sat down. She saw how respectfully he placed his body in the chair.

***

He closed his eyes, leaned back, and took several conscious breaths. He noticed the chair's design allowed the fingers to naturally align as they curled over the edge of the arm. Its smoothness invited a caress. As he rubbed his fingers gently over the surface, his body relaxed as if by magic. The seat fit his large frame perfectly as if made just for him. He followed her instructions and lovingly surrendered to its essence. Suddenly, an ancient tree form appeared to him, looking oddly human. Though startled, he held his focus. He tuned into its energy and felt a small, stabbing pain in his chest. Again, it surprised him, but he held his focus. The discomfort shifted, and a deep, inner voice told him that he was okay.

"I'm cutting some old tatters from around your heart. They've blocked my transmissions. There is much to teach you. If

you desire, I will help you to remember what you seek. Your genetics are unaware of me, but I will connect you to one of your oversouls. Relax, and allow the process."

Okay, thank you. I welcome your help. Abe replied. He continued his inner search. He could feel more connections being made. He continued caressing the arms of the magnificent being fused into the form of this comfortable chair. A face flashed in his mind, the craftsman, no doubt. He only saw the face for a second, but he would never forget it. He was sure of that. A wave of emotion swept over him. *Wow, brother, I remember you. You created this chair.* The tree's essence infused every fiber of the chair. He felt love for the tree that became this healing medium. His whole body vibrated from this dramatic revelation.

He opened his eyes and told Ty what he experienced. "I can't believe I sat in it before with no clue to its true presence. I noticed the carvings, yes, but I never really connected to it."

"No doubt it's been asleep since there's been no one to keep it awake by using it," she said. "It's been in hibernation for a very long time. I'll bet its creator designed this chair to be a healing chair. It told me earlier that it wanted to help me heal. I'll be taking advantage of it over the next few days."

"If it helps you, you certainly should," he said.

Suddenly, he remembered the soup, now way past done. After they ate, he cleaned up and said, "I need to help you get to bed." He reached for her bag, pulled out a candle, and lit it. While she held the candle, he picked her up and carried her through the rooms. "You take the bed. I'll sleep in the front room tonight."

She watched him gather his things. "I didn't mean to take your bed."

"That's okay, it's for only one night. Tomorrow, I'll have my own room. You gave me a workout today, so I'll have no problem going to sleep," he assured her. "One more thing I want to explain," he said as he helped her down the short hall to another door and opened it. The candle revealed an indoor privy. She stood there in disbelief. She took his arm for support as she hobbled over to a bowl with a hole in the bottom on a counter. "You plug it," he said.

"Hmm, that's smart," and then went over to a seat against an outer wall, molded out of clay like the countertops. Over in the corner, she saw a tub with something over the top of it. "What's this?" she asked.

"It's a stall. In the bottom, a hole allows water to drain."

"What's the box above it?" She looked at him to explain.

"It's a quicker way to bathe. I've tried it out and it's great. You fill this container up with heated water, and this slides so that water sprays over the top of your head."

"Hmm, interesting. That's a new one. Wow, no going to the outhouse. Back home, we had a bathing house, too. It's all right here in one room. Amazing! Where does the water come from?"

"Here, I'll show you." He reached for a handle that opened a small door in the wall, exposing the fireplace. "Through this sliding door, hot water can be handed through with a bucket. The fireplace has a metal pole that swings around. The hot water is dumped in a bucket and handed through this. Now let's go back to the kitchen," he said. Once in the kitchen, he pulled up a board on the counter and put the candle in the hole for her to see.

"Water," she said in awe. "There's water in there."

"Yes."

"Holy jiggers! We don't have to carry water, either?"

"No."

"Now that's amazing."

The buckets sit under the shelf here. There is also a metal container that you put on this rack to heat water over the fire pit. I guess it's a hot water well. At first, I couldn't figure it out, but I finally realized its width and saw that it must go here," he said as he crossed the short distance to the fireplace wall. "See how there is extra space here and why it's so wide. This explains it."

"Why isn't it already setting on the side of the fire?"

"I don't know. I guess it was put in storage under there."

"That makes sense."

"Anyway, I'll reset it at some point.

"Wow, they thought of everything." She turned to look at the basin for washing dishes. It also had a hole in the bottom to drain. She ran her fingers over the smooth surface. "This feels like pottery. How is this possible? You bake pottery to make it hard. This is rock hard," she said as she knocked again on the hard surface. "Holy jiggers!" She turned to examine the shelves. "This is utterly stupendous! I will love living here. They were far more advanced than any culture I am aware of. Who taught them all of this?" she asked.

"Good question."

"I can't wait to try this out." She examined every shelf and found a variety of metal kettles and pans, all a little old and crude. The carved wooden bowls and the pottery dishes revealed exquisite craftsmanship. "Everything is here just waiting for us to move in. Why did they leave all of this behind?" she wondered aloud. "You said everything about this place was a mystery, but why, I wonder." She looked down at a cluster of green stones that were embedded in the clay-like medium at the end of the cabinet. "What's this for?" she asked. "Why is it different from the rest of the countertop?"

"I wondered about that, also. It kept bugging me, so I asked one day. When I closed my eyes, I saw veggies and fruit laying on the cabinet with a beautiful, dancing energy encircling it all."

She ran her fingers over the smooth green surface that slightly rose out of the clay. "I wonder. Back home, we always put some stones around veggies after they were picked. I bet that is why these stones are here. They're permanent."

"I'll bet you're right. I can't believe I didn't think of that."

"Did your family talk about this?"

"Oh, yes. My mother would create an energy pattern over everything she picked and set them on stones she selected." He walked over to some stones that sat on the cabinet and brought them over to her. "She used these, and she made me bring them with me. We've always kept that understanding, and it sounds like your family did, as well."

"Yes, we did," she said. "This was our way of blessing, honoring, and respecting the plant forces that gave their energies to our bodies. Their gift transformed them into a new embodiment within us and enhanced our life force. I brought mine, too."

"Well, I guess we can put our stones with these. Do you know what gemstone it is?" he asked.

"I think it's emerald. My gramps had one the same color." She chuckled.

"What's so funny?"

My gramps wouldn't let anybody have it because he valued it so much. He said it was a gift from the ancient Goddess. He told lots of stories about it, so we always tried to get it from him. He would only let us hold it if we sat right by him. To him, it was priceless." She smiled. She reached into her pocket and pulled out a green chunk.

Tears started falling down her cheeks as she remembered her gramps putting it in her hands when she was getting ready to leave for the trip.

"He gave it to you?" Abe asked?

"He said it needed to go back home. You see, in one of his stories, he said the Goddess lived here. Each generation passed this down through time. He gave this to me so that it could go home. I told him it needed to stay with him, but he said it had to go back with me. "You keep it safe for me, for our family," he said. "It is yours now. When you reach Zathera, it will reconnect us back to our roots. With you being there, it will be as if we are there with you, child."

"That was a great gift," Abe told her softly.

"Yes," she said, placing it in his hand. He held it up against his chest and closed his eyes.

"Wow, this has a strong pulse to it."

"Yes, it has a long white glowing cord that kept its connection to here. The elemental kingdom is still strong in it."

Abe reached over with his other hand and placed it on the matching surface.

"Yes, it's the same energy." He felt a jolt ripple through him as the energy of the small stone woke up the stones on the countertop. "This smaller one just reactivated the plate here. They've been asleep. It's like a charging plate," he told her.

"I guess we've answered our first question. One riddle solved," she said as she sniffled and dried her tears away. "I miss my gramps."

Abe pulled her into his embrace. "I know, I miss my family, too. Now it's time to go to bed."

***

She pulled herself out of his arms. "Yes, you're right," she yawned. The day came crashing in on her. "I have much to process. I just realized that I don't have to figure it all out now, so I'm ready to go to bed." He helped her to her room and left the candle with her. She found her backpack sitting on the bed. She wondered what kind of softness it would have. The old one back home made sleeping uncomfortable. They stuffed it with layers of pine needles, and if they could find moss, they would put a layer of it over the top. It created a softer place to sleep. She wondered what Abe used. The frame of the bed showed the same beautiful craftsmanship as the chair.

She pushed down on the bedding to try out its flexibility. To her surprise, there was a give to it. She tried to pull back the material that covered it, but it wouldn't come up. She thought perhaps Abe left a blanket behind for her, but it wasn't. Something permanently covered it. "Oh, well, it's comfortable," she decided. She might check it out better in the morning. Another riddle to solve. "What's in it?" she asked the invisible spirit of the house. All the clothes she owned were there in her backpack. She found a place for everything in the cabinet, then realized Abe might want her extra bedroll.

"Abe, you can use my bedroll for some extra softness."

"That would be nice," he yelled.

"Come on in."

"Okay."

"Do you need to use the privy?" she asked.

"No."

"Okay, I'll use it then."

"Here's a bucket of warm water. I thought you might want to clean up. I should re-check your bandage," he said.

When he finished, she tried to wash out as much dried blood from her face and hair as she could. Abe brought a kettle in so she could soak her bloody tunic. The blood ran down her head and all over her collar and sleeves. "I may never get rid of all these blood stains. Looks like my old traveling clothes may never be the same." She scrubbed at them. *At least it matches the red of my tunic.* She inspected her brown-colored pants, badly torn from the fall. *I'll need to do some patching to repair the tears,* she thought, *but overall, they look salvageable.* She looked forward to going to the pool to fully wash her hair. She checked her bruised and swollen ankle. *Thankfully, it's not as painful as it could have been. I'll make some more tea tomorrow.*

Abe helped her back to the bedroom and told her he had some smudging herbs that could help her body recover from the trauma. "Would you be open to trying them?"

"Sure, I'm familiar with smudging."

He found a metal bowl for the hot coals, dropped some dried herbs on it, and walked out.

"Thanks," she told him as he closed the door. She undressed and lay down in bed, grateful for this happy ending to an eventful day.

11. Day One at Zathera

She woke in a slight panic but then remembered, *I'm here, I finally made it*. She lay with her hands on her belly and started her morning ritual to manage her energy levels. She thanked the sun, the earth, and the bed that allowed her to enjoy her night's rest. She thanked the spirit of Zathera for her new home. She hoped her parents received her telepathic message that she made it to Zathera safely. She consciously aligned her energy with that of Zathera. Once she completed the ritual, she tried to get up, but her head and leg screamed at her to stay in bed a little longer.

She reached for her medicine pack and pulled out two small bags of stones. She sat in bed and emptied them in front of her. She loved this medium. It would tell her what she needed for the day. Each amber stone had various glyphs carved on it. She arranged them to create a sentence. One by one, she deciphered the symbols that represented the energy from her sleep state to integrate with her waking life. Through her heart's door, she helped bring spirit into her physical body to raise its vibrations. Sometimes she would draw them out one at a time, but not this morning. She asked if another set of stones might offer better help. *Yes,* she heard, so she picked up the other bag and dumped the black stones in front of her. She had to be careful with these softer stones because the black powder easily rubbed off.

Oh, yes, these are for going through the gateway, she intuited. Most were planetary symbols to realign her various bodies. *Thanks for your help, Light Codes*, she thought, and set them on the floor.

Yep, there is no reason to rush to get up. She grinned to herself. *Truthfully, it's him that I want to see, but he can wait. He's not going anywhere.* She realized that she needed to take it easy and rest a lot today, so she laid back to do just that. She dozed off but awoke, realizing that she needed to relieve herself. She slowly got out of bed and hobbled quietly down the hall. Afterward, she returned to bed and fell asleep again. A knock on the door brought her back to consciousness. She woke in a daze, confused by her surroundings. Her head quickly cleared, and she yelled, "Yes, what is it?"

"I have something for you to eat."

"Come on in." He set a tray of fruit, some bread, and some slightly cooked mushrooms and vegetables in front of her. The extensive spread surprised her. "Where did you get all of this?"

"Oh, around," he said, smiling.

"You must have searched the woods to find all this."

"No, not really."

"I don't understand." Then she remembered the soup the night before. It also had a variety of vegetables that she didn't recognize due to their mushed, overcooked state. She never thought much about it last night, but looking at this brought it all back. She hadn't paid much attention to what he offered her then because of her hunger. Now, she could see a variety of squash new to her. Did it grow in the wild here? She couldn't make sense of it, but decided to let it go for now. She sang her usual mantra over it, thanking the food for giving her life, and ate it gratefully. "Did you already eat?" she asked him.

"No. I will in a little bit."

"Go get it and come and eat with me."

"Great," he said. When they finished, he asked: "How are you feeling this morning?"

"Grand, I'd say, compared to yesterday. I was a little fuzzy when I woke up. It took a few moments to clear the cobwebs, but now I'm feeling better. Thanks for asking."

"Do you feel that you're up to doing what we talked about yesterday?

"Oh, yes, I'm ready."

"Okay. Take your time getting dressed while I clean up the other room and fill the bed mat so I can sleep on it tonight."

"Sounds like a plan. You go, 'do the do' and I'll get ready." He looked at her inquisitively. She realized what she said may have sounded confusing to him. "That's a saying my family used. It means go do what you have to do."

"Oh, that makes sense." He turned to leave and then stopped, "What a catchy phrase. I'll go 'do the do,'" he said as he chuckled and left the room.

She wiggled herself back down into a lying position and acted like she had just woken up. She wanted to finish her morning routine because it was the way that she set up the energy for the day.

Good morning, self, she said. *I'm in my sacred space, and I declare that I own my day and everything that transpires in it. I choose to be fully present in each moment. I am waking up and becoming a conscious, evolving, Divine human. I love my physical body, the body I, as Spirit, chose to put on and live my Life in."* She rubbed her hands all over her body to thank it and share her love and gratitude for everything it did for her. *I love you! I love you as me,* she said as she hugged herself, *and I love who we are giving birth to. I am grateful for this day and everything I have. I also devote this day to learning, growing, and nurturing my integrated being.* After several integrating breaths, she declared, *so be it. Now, I've set my day in motion.*

She needed to process her dreams and the codes from the stones and apply them to her waking life. Her head still hurt, which may have affected her wild and crazy dreams. This strange place also affected her, and she still felt disoriented from her fall. Without thinking, she rubbed her belly. *Good,* she thought. Her grids experienced a lot of changes. *No wonder I feel so discombobulated.* The Earth grid she had lived on since childhood no longer supported her. It would take her physical body over a week to adjust to this new grid. She needed to create a new normal for her waking life.

She felt herself weaving in and out of several realities. She went back to revisit her outer Abe aspect that also reflected her inner male. All her various bodies needed to shift to integrate his new influence on her life.

She needed to accept responsibility for all these new aspects of her life to consciously archive what happened and bring her energy field up to date. Yesterday, she had been so out of it that she forgot to do this. She must create her omni-mind, one separate from the collective consciousness of this external reality. She breathed this awareness through her. She understood the time had come to interface with the heart of Zathera. She examined her energy to see if her experiences under Zathera's energy dome had become fully integrated. *Am I done now?* she asked her body-mind. The energy settled down in her gut, and she felt grounded. She took several deeper breaths to help with all of the dimensional changes. *Can I get up?* she asked her body. *You do feel so much better now.*

She learned over the last year or so that if she didn't take the time to process everything before her feet hit the floor, later she might wish she had. She grew so sensitive to energy that if she didn't keep on top of it and keep it clear, it would create backed-up pressure, especially in her gut, causing pain and discomfort. She couldn't allow that now. Setting up her intentions for the day allowed her to keep the energy flowing throughout the rest of the day. She never really knew how the day would evolve, but she knew this process worked. There had been a time when she couldn't eat and could barely even drink water for weeks on end. This made her dig until she figured out how to keep her energy streams clear and moving.

She learned to listen to her inner guidance and create a clearing procedure. She felt it saved her life. Now, she felt a little more like a normal person. *My Omni, I love you and thank you so much for helping me learn to manage my energy flow.*

Okay, on with the day. I am so excited about this new day. She tried to slowly rise.

She put her feet on the floor and reached for her bag. *Boy, am I moving in slow motion today.*

That's okay, body. We can do it. There's no rush.

She slowly hobbled into the kitchen and sat in the carved chair. She loved looking at the grandness of the magnificent, old hearth and the stonework that covered that side of the room. A specialist who knew how to create patterns in stone designed it with great artistic flair. She allowed herself to go into its energy. The pattern resembled a stone labyrinth. She noticed a smaller trail of rough gemstones embedded amongst the larger stones, barely visible to the naked eye. She hobbled over to the hearth's stone ledge, which nearly came up to countertop height in front of the tall fireplace, and sat down. *It's a great addition to the design of a fireplace. Not so much bending over. Hmm, that was a good idea.* The stone seat still felt warm from Abe's fire last night. She placed her palms on it and lovingly caressed its beauty like she had done with the chair the night before. She developed this habit to honor and respect anything that came from Mother Earth as an extension of oneself.

She felt the familiar response. Its energy woke from a very long nap. *Wake up, wake up,* she called as she sang to it. An old energy stirred within the walls of the whole dwelling. She felt some of it awakening, but a deeper force had not yet stirred. Something began to form on her inner screen.

Welcome back, it said, followed by a long yawn.

Thank you, she responded to the voice.

So, you have finally returned, came back the gruff, old voice.

Y-yes, we have, she replied, taken aback by the stern tone.

Wait. *What do you mean, I have returned?*

You are the mistress of this dwelling. I should know because you used to live here long ago with me.

I did?

Yes, you both did.

So, you knew he was already here? she asked.

Yes, the voice said slowly.

She struggled to understand the slowness of his response.

I, the heart of this dwelling, had not yet been awakened.

You just did that for me. Thank you.

She glanced at the energy of the hearth. Energy began lighting up both levels of the stone pattern. The remaining embers in the fire glowed and energized the invisible gemstone trail that spread across the face of the stone wall. *Now, it is awake,* she said to herself with a deep breath.

As she sat on the side of the hearth, she consciously infused her breath with the activated energy trail and connected to the whole spirit of the dwelling. Whatever vitality infused these walls would be nourished by this energy. All the energies of the stones, crystals, and trees that gave their life to take on this form merged so they could live within the human experience. She shot the energy outward to connect with the rest of the grid that now awakened through Abe being there, too. All of this would nourish and support the human inhabitants. The heat from the fire warmed the spirit and the soul. Food on this hearth would have a new form, a new energy for the body to experience. "Wow," she said. She could feel a new perception coming through. Being here at Zathera brought back a forgotten awareness she had once known. The realization that they would both live here together now shoved itself to the forefront of her consciousness. With it came a quiet peace and a clarity of purpose. Every part of her was being vibrated with this knowledge. They came back together after being separated for many lifetimes.

Just then, Abe walked in with his arms full of a big cloth he had tied together so he could carry his bundle into the cabin. He dropped it on the table, went back outside, and returned with another bundle, which he left on the cabinet by the sink. He came over and sat down. He was breathing heavily. He got up and reached for a cup, filled it up in the water well, and returned to his seat. After he caught his breath, he asked if he could do anything for her.

"Yes, I would like to have some more tea just like yesterday's."

"Sure." He got up and poured water into the kettle. He used a stick to stir up the coals and placed some kindling over the hot embers. With the flames burning brightly, he put some bigger pieces of wood over them and swung the kettle over the fire.

He brought all her bags of tea from the cupboard so she could select her desired mixture of herbs. As she fumbled through them, he couldn't help but mention the dirty black bag that lay there with the other light-colored bags. "What is this one?" he asked as he slowly picked it up and held it out to her.

"Yeah, it does look dirty, doesn't it?" she said, making a face. She hesitated for a moment, wondering if he would accept what she had to say.

"Tythea, you should know by now that it's okay to speak your mind around me."

"I guess so," she said, a little uncertain. "Ok, it's all black because of what's in it. I don't know if your family kept this old tradition up, but we have. We take this because we learned long ago it is a way to help the body detox and stay grounded with the earth. If we do this at least once a week, it helps to counterbalance the effects of the polarization in our genetics that tries to keep us in our heads."

"Yes, of course," Abe said with a smile across his face.

"You're talking about a special blend of Charcoal?"

"Yes."

"I keep mine in that wooden box," he said.

"How often do you take it?"

"My body likes it twice a week."

"To an average person, this sounds strange, and they'd poke fun at us, wouldn't they?" she asked with a smile.

"Yes, they probably would."

She turned back to her pile of herbal bags and she chose several. She made her mixture and gave her bowl to him to pour in the boiling water. As they sat there, she told him about experiencing the spirit of the cabin.

"Wow! What an awesome experience."

"There is another aspect I left out. It told me that I am the mistress of this dwelling and that we once lived here."

"Well, that's confirmation," he said as he smiled.

"Why?" This making sense to him surprised her.

"Some part of myself remembered it because I chose it out of all the other buildings.

"Amazing! Good validation."

"I also saw the energy of the stones around the hearth. Have you noticed the smaller gemstones kind of mixed in around the bigger stones?"

"No, not really." He frowned.

"Why the frown?"

"You noticed something I didn't. The beauty of the larger stonework drew me to it, but I never examined it as deeply as you did."

"Well, I've been taught this. I guess you weren't. I'm sure you know things I don't."

"Yeah, I guess so. So, what did you see?"

"Amongst all the larger stones, there is a hidden pattern. Go over there and gaze at the stones with an open mind and be aware that you are connecting into the spirit of this alive structure. Relax your gaze, don't focus, and ask to see the energy labyrinth in the stones."

He stood for some time studying the stones and finally yelled with excitement. "I see it!

Wow, there it is. But why would someone hide it? You don't need to hide it here."

"I don't know, but when I tuned into the fire energy earlier, it showed itself to me. It must have to do with how many elemental energies the builders wove together to create this place."

"They must have needed higher-frequency stones to blend with the other stones. I guess it's another one of those mysteries for now. Whoever built it knew these deeper secrets. In every dwelling, the hearth is your center place where everyone gathers. That's where the power resides for the whole family, right? We know that internally, and we also know that the outer home reflects the inner union, too. The chair first, then the hearth, the heart of the home. I wonder what else shows up for us."

"I guess we'll see in time," he said. "I guess the lesson for me is to be more present and observe things better. When I get busy, it's hard to focus on more than one thing."

"Oh yes, I know."

The water finally boiled, so Abe swung the kettle out and dumped the hot water into an old, cast-iron teapot.

Ty asked if he wanted to see what transpired between the stone pattern and the fire with the water and the herbs. "Tune in. All the elements are going to put on a show now that we know about them."

"Okay."

***

He went through the steps she gave him, and before he knew it, he could see the exchange. The whole wall glowed with sparkling energy. When he zoomed out a bit, he saw the grid that the building sat on. Energy flowed quickly. He turned his attention back to the fireplace and focused on the exchange there. The fire became more than a mere flame. Two different energies danced around it. Both around and within the flame an additional layer began to form in front of them. The flickering energy mesmerized him as it danced around in a spherical pattern.

"Look at the water," she exclaimed. "It wants to dance right out of the kettle spout as if it's trying to join the dance," she said with a giggle.

Then he noticed the essence of the herbs. The fire affected them as well. He could sense a pattern of white energy forming around the green leaves. It not only cradled the leaves but also leapt upwards like the flames themselves. They took on a peculiar pattern reflecting their unique signature. The essence of the fire caressed the herbs, transforming their separate energies and fusing them through this dance into a completely new, natural signature pattern with the power to heal.

"Wow!" The show captivated him. He saw that the herbs now carried a new frequency spectrum. He opened his eyes. "This gives me a whole new perspective on what I'm eating and drinking here. It's utterly astounding to me. I knew we could change the energy of our food, but I've never seen anything like this before. Thanks for bringing this to my attention."

"So, what's in that bundle there?" she asked.

"While I was out looking for fillers for my bed mat, I found some food."

"That's a lot."

"Yes, it is."

"What did you find?"

He picked it up, laid it on the table, and slowly began to untie it.

She watched his playful mannerisms. "What are you up to now?"

He pulled back one corner and watched her expression change.

"Where did you get all this?" she asked in a bewildered tone.

"Oh, out in the garden."

"Out in the garden?"

"Yes, there is a garden here with all of this in it and more."

"Are you kidding me? Do you expect me to believe that there is a garden out there that has already been planted for us and is just there waiting for us to pick it?"

"Yes, I do. Here's the proof. Again, that's why I said that you wouldn't believe this place."

"Who planted it then?"

"I don't know. I think it replants itself every year."

"So, it's gone wild then."

"I wouldn't say that. It doesn't look like it's gone wild. I've done a lot of thinking about it. I understand there is a collective intelligence that's still here, gardening and doing the replanting every year. You know plants make seeds every year and they can come back up the next year."

"Yes, I know."

"Well, I think the elementals and the divas keep it alive from year to year. Here's another thing you will have a hard time believing. There are no so-called weeds anywhere in this garden. They are outside the perimeter but not inside."

"I am going to have to see that for myself. I've never heard of such a thing."

"I hadn't either until I came here. It took a long time to get used to that idea. There were plenty of times when I wished I never had to pull another weed. I hoped our intentional sacred space garden would work in that way, but it never did."

"You and me both," she said laughingly. "One more thing to see. Another mystery to be revealed and understood. The list keeps getting longer."

He turned back to the food: "Do you recognize any of them?"

"I think this is a type of squash."

"Yes, I've seen those. This one is good raw or cooked." He went through all of them, explaining what he had experimented with so far. "The soup last night had a lot of these in it."

She laid out all the food on the table. He'd gathered enough food for the next few meals. She would love to have some of her favorite cooking herbs and decided to check them out for herself when she was able to see the garden. "Are there many edible herbs in the garden?"

"Oh sure, there are a lot."

"Why didn't you bring any of them?"

"Because I don't know them like you do. I can recognize some but there are others I don't know."

"I'll have to check them out."

"I'll take you at some point," he promised. He fell silent as a faint smirk flickered across his face.

"What now?"

"Oh, nothing. I just remembered something that I think you will enjoy checking out."

"What?"

"No, I'll let it be a surprise," he said with a big grin.

"Another surprise to add to the growing list. I'll have to add another column." she chuckled.

He had another cupid moment. *She's in me,* he thought, *with every smile and every word she speaks. I'm falling for her big time. She's down-to-earth, she's smart, and she's all about healing. She's just so many things all rolled up in one. The more we're together the more I'm loving and respecting who she is.* He pulled himself back to listen to what she was saying.

"Can you put the rest of this stuff up on the shelf there and put the backpack over on those shelves by the back door?"

"Sure." He welcomed the few moments to finish his revelry. "Do you need anything else?"

***

"No, I'm fine." She hobbled carefully to the warm stones by the hearth and stretched out on them. She enjoyed the energy as it flowed through her body. She could feel the spirits playing around in her field helping with her healing process. *We are all so connected,* she said to herself. *I love you all.* She could almost hear their quiet laughter for being recognized and appreciated.

After a short rest, she thanked them, got up and returned to her room. She ran her hands over the stone wall behind her bed, still delightfully warm from the fire. She lay on the bed and raised her leg, propping it on the short bedpost to relieve the throbbing. She pushed herself too hard. She took some deep breaths to relieve the pressure in her ankle and re-centered herself in her sacred space. She asked her divine spark to re-adjust, re-align, and make whatever modification she needed on all her dimensional levels. When she finished, she placed her hands over her enlarged belly. "Where do you play into all this?" she asked out loud. *So many questions I don't have answers for. I am on a personal quest to get answers for myself. I just need to trust a little longer. My guidance never leads me astray.*

She thought back to a conversation with her parents. She brought up a message she had received telling her to go to Zathera without delay. They had concerns about her going off into the wilderness alone. They worried that being pregnant for the first time might make the journey too hard on her. However, they encouraged her to go after her mother had a visitation revealing a higher purpose for this trip. Her mother's omnipresent voice told her that the divine promise of the return to Zathera was unfolding. *Let it run its course. This ancient prophecy must be fulfilled. You have nothing to fear. Everything will work out and one day you will understand what it's all about.*

She told Ty that she would make this trip for all of humanity. Ty admitted being scared to go off into the unknown by herself. After she dealt with those fearful thoughts, she knew she had to go on this quest no matter what. This trip involved the child growing inside her. She could do this because of her strong faith in the guidance she received. She felt strong gratitude for her integrated, sacred dream body guiding her all along the way. She remembered as a child she consciously created a connection with her divine double. She saw it as a child. Ever since then, she allowed it to guide her every step. It pulled her forward in life.

As she held her belly now, she sent love to what she carried inside of her. She still didn't understand everything, but she allowed this miracle to be expressed in whatever way it needed. For the first several months, she doubted many times what happened to her, but it was her Ta'non'ya essence that would show itself as being real. *"I allow, I allow,"* she told herself once again. *I must allow it. If I don't then I would be disowning myself, who I am, and what I've experienced. I know my connection, and I trust it. Therefore, I allow this."* With this daily re-consecration made, she closed her eyes to rest.

12. The Secret Behind Trees

She woke with a start. As she lay there, she realized she might not be able to conceal her bulging tummy if she got wet. They talked about it being hard to believe all these mysterious things going on about this place, but if she told him her story, would he believe in her immaculate conception? She knew it would be a test, but she felt in her heart that he would pass it.

Ty got up and walked down the hall and found Abe sitting in the carved chair.

"Did you have a good nap?" he asked.

"Oh, yes, I slept like a log. How long was I out?"

"Quite a while."

"Is your room all done?"

"Yes," he said. "I've opened all the windows except yours so that the breeze can blow all the dust out that I stirred up. I'll go open yours now."

When he returned, Ty asked him to pour some tea for her.

As she drank the tea he asked: "When do you want to go through the entrance and to the spring?"

"I'm ready now if you are."

She went to her room and changed clothes. She came out with a shorter version of what she wore earlier.

He grabbed a large drying cloth while waiting for her. He helped her to the door and closed it behind them. He swooped her up in his arms. "Are you ready?" He looked her in the face. Before he realized it their lips met ever so gently. He knew there was more to come. He slowly raised his head and whispered, "I'm falling for you."

"And, I'm falling for you," she replied with a sigh.

"Good," he smiled.

That smile could melt any cold heart, she thought. *When he smiles, his inner light shines through his eyes like the sun, and his soft, warm lips yield to whatever I desire.*" She felt his openness to please and knew it came with no strings attached. *This man is a keeper*, she thought, *a real jewel.* Each soft kiss stirred a rising warmth within her.

"I know we are meant to be together," he said.

"Yes," she said softly. They smiled at each other as she anticipated more to come.

"Let's get going on our adventure, shall we?" he asked quietly.

"Yes, let's go for it".

"I've explored almost all the buildings, so I'll be your guide," he said. "Trust me if I don't show you everything today. There's a lot to see, but we don't have to go through all of it in one day."

"Since you are carrying me around, I will try and behave," she said with a mischievous smile.

"You better, girl." As their playful words bounced back and forth, he gave her a quick peck on the cheek. He reminded her that they were headed back around to the original road so they could come up to the front entrance, which they had avoided the night before.

He carried her along the side of the stone circle, crossed the small bridge, and walked through the meadow to the far end. As they walked up the old road, Abe had to dodge around some rutted ground. *Obviously, there had been little attention paid to this abandoned entrance;* she thought.

"Is the rest of the road this bad?" Ty asked.

"Yes."

"I guess that's why you found it easier to take the trail we used."

"Yes, for sure."

They rounded a corner, and she could see the entrance ahead of them.

"Wow! OH," she said in a strained voice.

"What?"

"The minute I saw the gate I felt as if something hit me in the gut."

"Oh, that. Yes, I felt it as well."

She refocused herself as her midsection began to quiver slightly. With each breath, she gradually brought herself back into alignment as they continued through the transition zone.

***

Abe stumbled a bit. His feet and legs suddenly felt exhausted, like walking through deep water up to his waste. Even conscious breathing didn't help, so he stopped to figure out what he needed to do before they went any farther. He noticed a fallen tree they could sit on.

She opened her eyes as he veered off the road. Before she could ask a question, he told her he needed to rest his legs.

"Good," she told him. "I need some time as well."

He turned his attention to the symptoms they both experienced. Abe stretched out on the ground because his abdomen hurt so badly. When he finally sat up, Ty seemed to be feeling better. He told her his experience.

"I'm not surprised."

"Why?"

"Because you were carrying me and anchoring your experience from two nights ago. Together, we had to forge a trail of codes bringing our two paths back together. We outwardly represent what each person must do within themselves. As we came back together, we dropped the external grid that supported us in the past. We created a completely new one. Your legs felt that weight because you represent the male species that's not been connected to their feminine side. On a genetic level, we are programmed to be disconnected. Being a man, your female side had to be reconnected on an energetic level. I represent the feminine side that's felt disconnected from her inner male side. I felt it in my upper diaphragm. Together, we are helping ourselves reconnect by supporting and honoring each other."

"Yes." He felt the joy of the reconnection. "It feels right. Are you ready to proceed?"

"Yes, I am," she said, smiling.

He swung her into his arms, sneaked a quick kiss, and headed towards the gate.

"I feel so much better now that I shifted through the gunk," he said.

"I do, too. It's weird how we both experienced such a huge reaction here. More than any of the other Rings. I want to tell you something I've been hearing."

"What is it?"

"Two words: shared heart."

"What do you think it means?"

She was silent for a moment. "I think it means that together we represent a unified heart consciousness. We both found our way home by understanding that it is our own, indwelling presence. Our heart guided us to this inner gateway, our heart's portal that leads us to a new dimension of ourselves. Also, last night I dreamt that I walked through this long white tunnel, but at the same time, I watched it from the outside. I viewed this wonderful experience from both sides. The tunnel is the energy trail we went through to get to this gateway. It also represents the inner door of our hearts. Remember, they reflect each other."

"Just like 'as above, so below.'"

"Exactly."

A grand, silvery-white wooden arch stood in front of them. It created a wide gate spreading across the entrance. "Look at the detail of that carving," Ty said, sharing her thoughts.

Two magnificent, twin trees and matching large emerald stones also framed the entrance like guardians. The silver sheen of the arch made a beautiful contrast to the huge trees looming overhead. They could see an unusual script etched into the arch and at the ends were matching crests. "How did they do that?" she asked.

"What?"

"The arch is massive. How is it still there after all this time? The silver color looks new. It still sparkles.

He looked at her with amusement.

She smiled at him. "It's another mystery, isn't it?"

"Yes, you learn to take it in stride around here. It intrigued me at first, too, but the more I looked around, the more normal it seemed," he said.

"It would be a welcome sight for any tired traveler that made it this far."

"Yes, as it was for me. Are you ready to walk through on your own without my help?

"Yes, please." He lowered her to the hallowed ground.

Her feet stood on the ground at the entrance to Zathera for the first time.

"You should feel yourself shift into a place like you've never experienced before in this body. However, it should feel familiar."

"I know I've lived here before," she said. "I wonder why I didn't feel anything special about being here last night."

"Because I carried you and helped support your energy," he replied. "I don't think you connected into the core at that time. By entering on your own two feet, you rightfully entered the Gate Way of Zathera and its true spirit centered here in the hub."

"That makes sense," she said. "And it helps me understand something I felt before."

***

Touching the road's grid made her feet tingle. A tunnel of light opened before her inner eye composed of a fabric woven with multi-colored energy lines. "Oh, my gosh," she said. The lines went through her and connected her to the grid field of the dome over Zathera.

All the many spider webs she had ever seen came to mind, but this one topped them all. *Oh, if I could only draw this!* she told herself. She stood there, bathing in the energies wrapping around her. "I surrender all that I am so I can return home," she proclaimed. She shuddered from head to toe as this magical realm invited her to enter.

Suddenly, she saw herself in the center of the column of light. A burst of warmth spread outward from her heart. She focused on her breath until she felt one with the golden light stream. A loving feeling rushed through her as this new realm welcomed her home. She relaxed and disappeared into its essence, feeling united with the intelligence that created this realm. After some time, she returned to her normal awareness, standing on the road. *Normal.* she thought. *No, I'll never be the same again.*

She became aware of her feet, the ground beneath them, and the arch above her head. Zathera accepted her as one of its own. With Abe's support, they walked under the webbed energy rings surrounding this place. With each step, she felt more at home and even lighter as she moved farther inward. *This is home,* she thought. *I know beyond a shadow of a doubt that I have lived here not just once but many times which explains why I am having such a strong, overwhelming experience."*

Pangs of discomfort flowed up her legs. Her physical body struggled to get used to this new space. *It might take a few days to align my past with my present circumstances,* she thought. She breathed to clear any remaining debris in her fields while spinning her energy until the intensity of her discomfort subsided. It continued decreasing as she got to the other side of the gateway.

She told Abe about her experience. "Thanks for your help."

He placed his hand over hers. "I'm glad I could help. I experienced exactly what you did, and it's something I'll never forget."

"It was remarkable."

She drank in the whole village from where they stood like a thirst that couldn't be quenched. "It's so beautiful!" She inhaled deeply the sweet fragrances from rose bushes and other flowers and shrubs lining the road and scattered throughout the village. "Oh, I love roses and flowers. Everything is so beautiful right now. I can hardly see our cabin from here." She sensed the elementals everywhere.

She marveled at the arched bridges and the unusual stones that lined the river. "The design of the village is out-of-this-world."

He pointed out several of the buildings he previously explored.

"It feels like I'm home," she said as tears rolled down her cheeks.

"I know what you mean. Are we ready to start the next adventure?"

"Yes, I think I am." This experience opened her eyes to see Zathera in a new way. She wanted to pinch herself to verify the reality of what she experienced because it all made her feel so different. "Entering through the gate changes everything. These trees are so massive." She breathed it all in. "Ok, Abe, where to?"

"The Grand Hall." He scooped her up in his arms. "Now remember, we're just going to do a quick walk-through, okay?"

"Yes, sir."

The Grand Hall sat to the left of the entryway. Once they reached the bottom step, he lowered her to the ground. Something didn't feel quite right to her. Perhaps they needed to do something first. She felt compelled to turn and looked out at the park in front of them. "I'm asking my guidance if there's something we need to do before we enter." As soon as she closed her eyes and centered herself, it came to her. She opened her eyes so quickly it surprised him.

"Wow, that was quick."

"It was so close I could sense it but couldn't quite grasp it. I used my key to hone in on it, and it worked."

"What is it?"

"It's about the tube of light that we both saw. The column goes through the gateway creating a wormhole, but where is the actual center? All the outer Rings of Light must energetically converge here. We need to attune ourselves to this alignment, which must be nearby. Something is grounding it, but where?" She directed her question to the elementals. "Show me," she yelled out into the unknown. "Did you feel the need to ground yourself when you came through the gate the first time?" she asked, turning to Abe.

"Not really. Okay, you've got my curiosity piqued. "Where is it?" he asked, putting his arms up in the air.

"I think we both need to tune in to sense it," she suggested. "I'm feeling a pull in that direction." She pointed to some giant trees and started walking towards them.

"Hey, girl, what did I tell you?" She stopped, and he swung her up into his arms.

"Over there." They walked across the old road to the towering trees in the distance, following the river that snaked its way through the heart of the village, passing buildings carefully landscaped in the natural settings along the way. Whoever designed all this intentionally kept everything in harmony and balance. She loved it.

Something nearby insistently caught her attention. *What is it? Where is it?* she asked herself. She closed her eyes, *okay, body, you be my guide.* She started turning her body like a divining rod. "Light, the central tube of light. It's not coming from the sun because the sun is not at the right angle. Over there," she pointed. "Did you sense that?"

He listened quietly to his guides, then pointed in the same direction.

"Yes!" she exclaimed.

He dodged several downed limbs to reach the spot. They stood with their eyes closed.

"There," they said in unison. A spinning field glowed in front of them.

"It's that tree," she said as her hand flew over her mouth. "Why would a gigantic tree be the catalyst in the middle of the village?"

"It looks like the tree itself is the grounding," he said.

She noticed his expression changed suddenly. "Is something wrong?"

He didn't answer at first. "I don't know. I feel something going on with me that I don't understand. Remember I told you my haunting dream about a tree spirit?"

"Yes."

"Well, here's the tree thing again. As a six-year-old, it scared me. It felt so massive. Even now as an adult, it's still overwhelming," he whispered. "My parents tried to help me but they didn't fully understand it. It's been a riddle my whole life. I'm still looking for an answer. Now here's this humongous tree staring back at me. It's the one from my dreams. It's like I'm six again. Intellectually, I know there's nothing to be afraid of, but I still need some understanding so that I can let go of my fear of trees. Maybe as we work with this, I can finally get some clarity."

"Abe, I'm getting that you might need to look at the tree from within so you can see it in a new light. It offers a spiritual message that will comfort your childhood fears when you learn it, but it's hidden behind your fear. You do what you need to do. I am going to the other side and hug it. Okay?"

She closed her eyes and slowly hobbled to the tree. The center of the wormhole aligned perfectly with its core. "Wow, you are gorgeous," she said to the tree. The spinning power of its force field became stronger with each step. She stretched her too-short arms around its gigantic trunk and sank into oneness with its massive force field.

Using her breath again, she centered herself and aligned with its core. Her abdomen went into a state of hyper-sensitivity, an indicator that she needed to ground herself through this massive being. A surge of strength shot up her spinal column, giving her some welcome relief. *I am one with you. I am one with me. I need what you offer me. I stand as one with this magnificent giant. Oh, Tree Being, I thank you for who you are.* This ancient creature represented the central pillar of life, one life for all, all the earth and the universe. She realized that the dome field over this whole mountain mirrored the canopy of a tree and reflected the way spirit overshadows even her own body.

Suddenly, a new download swept away old cobwebs clouding her vision. *This tree is a symbol of our inner connection to Source, as well as the outer connection that we lost.* The realization comforted her. *Most of humanity has been sucked down into lower levels of density. They have forgotten the inner path of oneness when everyone had been connected to the All That Is. This tree is making an extraordinary effort to regain that state.*

Originally, people had not been created as female or male. They were androgynous. She understood this. Genetic manipulation by extraterrestrials created the Adamic race of females and males. Sexual reproduction allowed the extraterrestrials a much quicker and easier method to control humanity, a species they needed. Consequently, human survival signals became disrupted.

Ty's culture understood humanity as the by-product of this experimentation. Their goal must now be to find a way to heal this split between humans and Source, and repair the damage to the body and its psyche. Each generation joined in this effort, so their bloodline never forgot its union with the universal Spirit. But intermarriage between cultures diluted their commitment. They fought a battle with the evolving mental body.

This became the Zatherian mission. But how best could they accomplish this goal? Thousands of universal entities agreed to come into physicality to help implement a plan to reverse the damage and heal the split. Creating the sexes was permitted but what followed after that was not foreseen. How to instill the light of love and understanding in humans became the goal. This meant we needed to come into a body to figure out this riddle. A new divine human template was needed. The plan required unconditional love on the part of both parties which meant laying aside their egos in favor of compassion to understand each other. *We must resurrect the original template of the Life Tree,"* she thought, *"if we are to become one again. We will have to find our inner spark and trust its guidance. We will have to release our feminine side from the repression it's been under because it will take the mother principle to revive the body consciousness it once had. With a repaired body, spiritual self-awareness, and personal guidance based on attunement with our inner spark of intelligence, the Source would be enabled to rise again out of the ashes of forgetfulness. With love, we will re-embrace our oneness.*

She now understood why Abe felt haunted by someone. The haunting came from his lost omnipresent self. He knew it and worked on it, but his body needed to heal the pain of being torn from its eternal Oneness. Finding itself set apart from its inner lover damaged the male. She could see that in a sense he felt abandoned. This sense of loss lay buried in his subconscious. She understood his remembered pain of being pulled away and left alone, just like the female had been ripped from her lover's embrace. Ty understood the greater difficulty most men experience in finding the way to their hearts and releasing the need to mentally judge their counterparts compared to women. To accept one another unconditionally challenged them both. She'll stay at his side while he finds a way to heal the old genetic scars of separation for the collective male condition. They both needed to release the hold of egos on them and return to true love which meant working energetically on the inside to consciously re-embrace the missing part of themselves. Rebirth is possible when one becomes aware of the imbalance within. Spiritual maturity opens the possibility to choose to heal the genetic split. Their culture realized the key to healing this wound and restoring harmony and balance to their lives lay in unconditional love, it was the missing key. It held the codes for healing.

Okay, now that I am aware of this, I can return to my Life Tree which represents my ancient roots in my divine self. This tree symbolizes a reflection of the wholeness of the universe in me. Now I see why I needed to put all this together, so I can archive this as I return. I went out there for a time, but now I represent the return to self as my source. The Sacred Tree stands as this symbol for us as we go on this journey of self-discovery. I wonder why a tree and not an animal or something else? She felt something shift inside as new data flooded her mind.

A beautiful, majestic tree appeared in her inner vision. As her perception deepened, she realized it represented one of the most ancient life forms created by the spirit of Gaia. The tree spirit showed her its legacy. As she hugged the tree, she felt a stream of energy from the giant. "I shift myself," she whispered. "I let go and allow." Thoughts started coming to mind as if the tree dictated them to her.

13. The Zibor's Message

Greetings. I am the Spirit of the Zibors, the Standing Giant Clan, known to you as the Tree Kingdom. I represent a collective that served as a bridge for you to enter physicality. We love and support our mother Gaia. We agreed to stand here to establish a connection between the Universal Spirit and the physical human spirit once more. You humans call this union omnipresence. We are the guardians here, and we hold this structure over Zathera for you. Our shadow represents the canopy enveloping this mountain. We have watched you and evolved with you. We are part of your past, present, and future. We ground this wormhole so that we can continue to grow along with you.

You may wonder how this is possible. In your distant past, we enjoyed a different relationship with you. We joined forces with the young original species during Zathera's creation. At first, we existed in a state of hibernation, like your Omnipresence has.

When the aliens altered you, it affected us, too. We no longer functioned as a bridge for you. Later, as you began to wake up, we found that you subconsciously remembered us, so we interfaced with you and your bodies again.

During the microbial stage of life on your planet, Gaia's spirit came to us and asked if we would help with her creation. You see, we represent the first variation of a womb, the first outer support for life in matter. Originally, we existed as both the mother and father of your physical bodies.

Later, another gift came from off-planet to form the next stage of life. The second one morphed us, turning us upside down. The second stage connected you to the Sun universal forces, what would be called the Wombs Within.

Can you see the resemblance? Look at your body. You resemble a tree that walks upside down. It's a brain twister isn't it. Your canopy or brain's nervous system keeps you rooted in the earth. Your skin soaks up all the solar forces of life like the canopy of leaves. Your heart center flows through the tree trunk that circulates all these forces from end to end. This was the original model for Life, one end rooted in the earth, the other open to the sun's forces. This created the proper balance. Life flows end to end in a circular pattern, the unending loop of Life. Your modified template became polarized, and duality set in. This forced you to look outside of yourself. You quickly destroyed the bridge we held open for you to the universe. Your spiritual genetics became hidden from you, and we lost our connection with you until a few of you threw off the old garment put upon you.

We stood all these eons watching you grow and evolve as a species. We know your joys and pains, your achievements and failures. We love you just the same. If we as the Standing Giants had any words of wisdom to pass on, we would tell you to take your power back and feel your inner strength and self-esteem, once again. You lost the ability to stand tall knowing who you are. You act lost, stumbling around in the dark. When they altered you, they disempowered you, snipping away at your spiritual genetic limbs. Their pruning dethroned you from your natural birthright. You need to continue genetically reversing the damage. Only then will we stand tall in you once more. Our gift to you is this: to allow you to stand upright, to become the whole person you are meant to be. We have complete faith in you.

Wake up. Wake up and reclaim your legacy. Remember, we are a part of you. We offer you our strength. Come back inward in your sleep time. Come back and curl up in our ancient arms. We can cradle you in your re-birthing womb, which remains there waiting for you to remember how to use it as a healing chamber. Use it to help with your modifications. We can share so many mysteries, if you embrace us, once more. Study our ways and our nature, love us in your trees, build a bridge where we can meet. Loving them activates a deeply hidden gene. Embrace us. Resurrect us in your spirit, in your heart, and mind. Learn to use our spiritual, rejuvenating qualities. Absorb our wisdom as you once did. Ask us to help, and we will remind you of all that's buried in your unconscious.

Ty frowned. She looked at Abe whose face also showed puzzlement.

I still sense some confusion, so I'll explain it this way. Long ago, we agreed to help our mother to manifest a new species. She asked for our help because this new creature needed to be modeled after a life form that had already gained awareness. We possessed several ingredients she wanted to incorporate in you. We agreed to help because until then, we were her greatest expression of an evolving presence that began to know itself in the plant kingdom. We represented the perfect balance she wanted. We stood tall in our inner integrity and strength. We survived all the storms, being so deeply grounded. The multiple layers of our trunk allow us to expand and grow while giving us the ability to protect ourselves from debris in the environment. Each layer develops as a universe unto itself, independent and yet bound together as one whole, symbiotic organism. Our unique central core, different from our surface layers, sets us apart from other plant life created by Mother Gaia.

It created a networking system that gave us the ability to be dimensional. I'm not saying that Gaia ignored other plants. The Mother merged many of their best properties to become a part of you. We were older, more mature, and could live a long time compared to the smaller, weaker forms of plant life. We evolved so many layers that strengthened the trunk and protected the unique central core, enabling it to maintain its purity against invasions attacking from the outer world. Our outer layers weren't aware that this core spirit could interface with them without their knowledge. This heart allowed us to become an interdimensional conveyor system. No other form ever evolved in this way. She recognized this as the perfect model she desired for you. She recognized our breathing capacity, so much greater than the smaller plants, yet another factor she wanted to incorporate into your bodies. Other plants freely exchanged their spiritual forces, but more on their outer edges. You can see it in their energy field while ours has an internal structure. The model that she created needed to have both energy systems, internal as well as external.

The one thing you need to understand is that when this new species was born, you needed space for both internal and external intelligence. One would contain the spirit of the planet, life spark, and the other would contain the universal flow of Spirit to cohabitate with a physical body. Both genetics needed separate systems, separate layers. Both aspects are needed to maintain life on separate levels yet able to merge and move within each other's realm.

We, the Zibors, evolved into the only Earthly species with co-existing layers. You experience us primarily in two ways: your skeletal structure and your skin. You stand strong and upright because of us. You possess several systems that pick-up energy, and you also draw life from the life of the universal sun that is connected to your core. The central sun shines as one of the major components from which you draw life. It's one thing to breathe like any other physical creature, but it's another to be able to draw life from all these layers at once.

Speaking in his deep, husky voice, he asked, *how do I explain this?* After a pause, he said, *here is the best example I can give you: your universal Spirit breathes and lives through your bones, the porous part of your bones, not just your lungs. Your planetary Spirit breathes through your lungs. Mother knew she needed something different than what she used before. Do you understand?*

Yes, Ty said, *that example gives me a better feel for it, thank you. So, are you saying that, when we were genetically modified, this deeper exchange in the bones came to a dramatic end?*

The Zibor continued. *Yes, very much so. When they cut you away from your source, this connection became severed as well. Communication stopped between the layers. Those signals became jammed.*

"Wow, this explains a lot", Ty replied. She took several deep breaths, calming herself to align with this new information. Holding her arms around the massive structure, she dug her fingers into the bark. *Oh, magnificent giant, I love and honor you. I choose to consciously connect to you within my spark chamber. I ask that you be activated in me. The road grew much harder without you, old friend, but I am glad to be in your loving embrace again.*

After several deep breaths, she felt a warmth flood through her. A vibration radiated out from her chest. It felt like her heart expanded to the bursting point. The intensity awakened a deeper resonant pulse from her primordial past as her body swayed to the rhythm of her mighty giant. "My heart now beats with yours," she whispered as she kissed the bark. She held her focus on the two harmonious rhythms. She thought, *wow, I can feel the tree's heart beating. Shared hearts that beat as one,* this realization hit her throughout her being. *Zibors, I will never forget this feeling.* She sensed the need to center herself again through her breath. *Yes, yes. I've done it! I've found my Zibor spirit. I'll never lose it again. I love you and thank you, Zibors, for making yourselves better known to me.* She dug her fingertips into the rough bark again and pushed herself away. She would never see trees in the same way again. She found a whole new level of respect for them.

Today has been quite a day, already, she thought. *I wonder what else might happen.* She turned around to look at Abe and found him waiting for her. She made her way over to him and sat down beside him on an old log.

"How did it go?" she asked.

"Oh, good. I went through a visualization that took me back to my spark's chamber and opened a new space to better understand the tree's symbolism. I know I'm a proxy for all men and their need to inwardly reconnect to their lost feminine side. I also know that a lot of other missing pieces need to be found for my energetic bridge to be repaired. Opening this space up will help me to create new circuitry for the males who follow. I decree and vow that we must heal our imbalance. How about you, what did you experience while you tried to hug the giant over there?"

"Yes, I tried," she chuckled. "Very funny."

"It was funny to watch you. Little ole' you trying to stretch your arms around that humongous trunk." He laughed.

"I can imagine what it looked like because I felt like an ant compared to the tree."

"You were gone a long time. What happened?"

She told him everything she experienced and the Zibors' message to them.

"Whoa! You did get a download."

"Yes, I did."

"It will take you a few days to assimilate all that."

"Yes."

***

"I'm starting to get a sense of the importance of these giants," Abe said. He chuckled as he remembered what he called them as a child. "I guess I did pick up on them correctly. I told my mother about the latest giant that visited me. I guess I'm finally letting go of my childhood fear of them. I wish they had talked to me like they did to you. Why do you think I couldn't receive them?"

"With them coming to you so young, perhaps you needed to experience this early on in life because of their importance to your mission. You didn't understand it at the time. You needed to walk it out as an integration process to bring this connection back online in you and for all men. Most of all, you needed understanding to restore this balance. My guidance tells me you must allow a space for new understanding. That's huge, and you've done it. Your growth guided you here to help me. That's another huge step for the male, to get past judgment. Together we choose to undo this damage done to our species. Don't forget what you've done. You've heard their guidance. Your dreams are proof of that."

He was silent for a moment. "You're right. I've just had different experiences than you. Same but different."

"Yes, yes," she said, touching his hand.

"Thank you."

"Glad I shared this with you. We both want to heal the injury, which we know requires a difficult journey through the inner darkness to the Source of our life. We shed our brain-bound limitations for the openness of our universal mind. I am doing the same as you, Abe, but I wish to repair, rebirth, and reconnect with my male aspect. Both of us desire not only to be open to accepting our missing piece and bringing it into balance within us but also to reconnect with our Omnipresence as a new mind to replace our old mental constructs."

"I know," she continued, "we will receive new insights into the nature of the tree spirits and why they're an important bridge for us. It requires a mind that's open to new and unusual concepts. We came back here to gain new information to complete the job we started long ago."

"That's good, Ty. I know some of what you're talking about, but you've added a lot more to it. The more you explain things, the more my consciousness expands. You know, this is so weird. I didn't understand that until the words came out of my mouth. Your words go straight to my heart." He put his hand on his chest to show her his feelings. "I know we're both doing this, but your words affect me deeply. Your outer presence strongly impacts my inner feminineness. It feels like you are inside of me. It's a riddle I will understand better as I walk it out."

"Yes, I'm sure you will."

"We've had enough deep stuff for a while. Let's have some fun now," Abe said with a big grin.

"Yes, but let's make sure we've finished integrating what we've experienced."

"Of course."

After they were done, Ty said, "I wonder what the rest of the day will be like?"

"Good question," he said flashing a grin. "I feel today is just the beginning of our new life together."

"Yes," she said, as a shy grin spread across her lips. He got up and reached for her hand to pull her into his arms. They stood looking into each other's soul for several minutes, then he lowered his head and gave her a long kiss followed by a long embrace.

"My lady, are you ready to go?"

"I am, sir," she said as she touched his cheek.

"Then, I am at your service. Let's go," and he picked her up.

"Where are we going, first?" she said, giggling in a playful way.

"Let's go back to the hall." He turned them in that direction.

"Gosh, that's such a huge building," she said.

14. Exploring the Grand Hall

The stone steps leading up to the grand hall caught their attention as they approached. A master craftsman poured all his love into his work. Above the three steps, an ornate stone patio provided a sheltered sitting area furnished with stone benches. "What's inside?" Ty whispered as Abe carried her up the steps to the weather-beaten doors.

Abe thought for a moment. "It reminds me of a wheel. There are five spokes to the design, some longer than others. On the other side of this first door is the large gathering hall. It leads to a community area in the center of the building. At the end of each remaining wing extending from the center, they built an exit with a nearby outhouse and an area for relaxation, like the central park area by the river. But why am I telling you all this? You need to see it for yourself. Let's go in."

"Of course," she said. "That's a no-brainer."

They didn't make it to the front door before he grimaced in pain. "Are you okay?" she asked.

"You mean the buzz in my head?"

"Yes, if you want to describe it that way."

"I get it every time I come through this entrance. I haven't figured out why. When I use the back door, I don't feel it, but I do when I come this way."

"You haven't explored why?" she asked, a little puzzled.

"No, I haven't taken the time, but I've learned one thing: this place differs dramatically from any of the other buildings I've explored. This whole building feels like it's alive. Notice, there is no decay like the place we're living in. This is unique. You'll see what I'm talking about. That's all I'm going to say for now. Are you ready to go on in?"

"Yes."

Before he could reach for the door, it suddenly swung open of its own accord. "See, I told you. It knows we're here." The dank, cool air hit them in the face.

"They shuttered the windows from the inside," Ty said, blinking. "I wonder why."

Abe sat her down on a bench by a table. "Sit here while I open some shutters so we can see and get some air moving through here."

***

A chill ran up her spine. She felt someone watching them. Her instinct told her to go back outside and come through the door without any help. Since he carried her in, she hadn't properly connected to the building's grid or the spirit of this structure. She learned that from the Zibors, as well as the spirit of the chair. *This place is a prime example of these structures morphing into a new form, a living, breathing body of intelligence. The building needs to be respected and acknowledged as such.* She felt the need to align herself to this new energy. *Master craftsmen created this building to give the tree forces an aesthetic, new form of expression. Like the healing chair, its master built this hall to allow the Zibors to offer more intimate service to their human companions. The Zibors guard this great hall.* So, she slowly and respectfully limped back through the doors.

"What are you doing?" Abe asked in alarm.

"I have to pass through the door on my own just as you did the first time." A long slab of emerald lay across the entrance. *Hmm, this must be the key—the key to its heart.* She respectfully acknowledged its presence: *I open my heart to you as you do to me,* and brought that awareness into focus as she entered.

Her feet started tingling as she entered the door and connected to the magnetic-electric field under the building, proving to her that this building carried a living intelligence.

Speaking to the great Being of the house Ty said, *I greet you with the utmost respect. I desire to connect with you so that I may know what you have become. I want to witness your grandeur, and experience who you are in this new expression. May I re-enter where I once lived so I may know you as you are today?* As she waited, she began to clear herself through the movement of her hands and holding her trinity triangle mudra. She scanned her body, gathered up any debris in her field, and shifted her energy to be compatible with this new form of the Zibors. *This does not feel the same as sitting in the living chair or hugging the giant tree.* She wanted to prepare herself to experience Zibor's life force in this immortal building.

From her sacred heart, in oneness with all that is, she accelerated her energy centers to purify any imbalance that might remain. *I am unconditional,* she decreed while breathing deeply and releasing her body to find a natural harmony with the life of the reborn tree beings. She felt their excitement that the two of them had returned. They opened the doors to welcome them in. The tingling sensation disappeared, replaced by a new clarity of mind as the ancient energy of the tree spirits slipped inside her. By stepping into this ancient structure, into the arms of the Zibor family, she felt them slip a shawl of protection over the shoulders of their human offspring, and her gratitude for them bloomed brighter.

"I wondered if they were going to let you get by with it," Abe said.

"What do you mean?"

"With you not entering the building on your own the first time."

"Why didn't you warn me?"

"The doors opened by themselves, so I thought they allowed me to carry you due to your injury. Plus, I knew you needed to have your own experience, so I decided not to say anything."

"You were correct. I needed to experience it on my own." She smiled, placed her hand over her heart, and bent her head slightly to indicate honoring his intuition: "Your intuition proved correct."

"Thanks," he said as he mimicked her gesture. "Are you ready to proceed?" With the shutters fully opened, the hall filled with light. He swung her into his arms and took her over to see one of the four massive fireplaces that lined the outer walls.

"This room could entertain a couple of hundred people," she said. A complex pattern in the stone covered the top half of the walls. She studied its pattern and felt a resonating pulse begin in her body. She couldn't quite figure out the pattern, but she felt its divine geometrical design.

The geometry of the patterns blended nature with symbolism. She took a deep breath to soothe the pulse moving through her. "I know I'm connecting to the Zibors as this structure, but I'm also connecting to another aspect that is part of the fireplace," she told Abe. She breathed it through and then turned to the bottom part. *True masterpieces. Not like anything I ever saw back home.* She studied the wooden trim, upward and around the room.

"Look, Abe," she pointed, "it frames all of the walls and even the ceiling." At the corner, elaborate carved swirls covered all three surfaces. Each corner had a matching pattern. She sensed that they were alive. "I've never seen anything carved so beautifully. The design matches the wood grain perfectly. But that's odd. Why would they need to match?" The trim along the floor showed a much simpler but just as skilled carving style. "Wow!" she said.

"It looks as if they planted vines in the corners, climbing upward to the ceiling and spreading along the crevasse where the walls and ceiling meet."

The corners created a decoration that enveloped the fireplaces.

"Everything interweaves into one masterpiece. It looks strange in a way," she said. "Yet it adds a wonderful energy.

Everything is brown but it feels green and alive to me. It's so calming and nurturing."

"Yes, I agree," Abe replied.

She felt the gatherings and the celebrations still hanging thick in the air. She could tell that the building still retained its memory of everything that ever happened under its roof, the festivities still etched deeply into the heart of the Zibors. Even after all this time, they held this relationship dear, and they felt great loneliness for human interaction. They delighted in the long-awaited return of humans. They entertained themselves and reminisced about the times they shared with their human family, yearning for their return. She shook her head and forced herself to shift out of these feelings. *Another time, she told herself, Not now. I'm running through enough energy as it is.*

She learned long ago not to take on too much energy at one time. It distressed her until she integrated it into her body. She chose to keep her energy balanced so she could eat and keep her strength up. A solid diet of energy didn't sustain her physical body well, something she learned the hard way.

"On with the show," she told Abe.

He picked her up and walked towards the far end of the gathering hall to a wall composed of several doors. "The doors can open or be removed completely. That opens everything up. They can be closed if need be."

"How clever."

"Yes, especially if you want to keep heat in." He sat her down, walked over to the doors, and swung two of them open. He picked her up, again, and went through the doors to the next room. They stood in a huge, circular area that resembled the commons area he'd mentioned before. With lower lighting levels than the last area, they could barely see down the hallway.

"Impressive," she said. One wing led to an open dining room. Beyond it, she vaguely made out a massive cooking hearth. Other hallways led in different directions. "What's down there?"

"Larger living quarters for adults and small families."

"There?" she asked, pointing down a different hallway.

"Rooms for the students."

"And there?"

"Classrooms. Several other rooms lie down in that corridor. There's also a laundry area that's mostly outdoors under a trellis."

She returned her attention to the room they stood in. "I can't believe all this furniture is still here. It's as if they just walked away and left everything behind." Old, dusty covers draped over everything. She noticed a row of windows along the south wall running to the ceiling. Despite a wide eve on the roof, light still streamed in. The eve sat at a slant so the sun could shine in naturally. "Great room. It sure invites you in. Even now it feels homey," she added.

15. The Apothecary

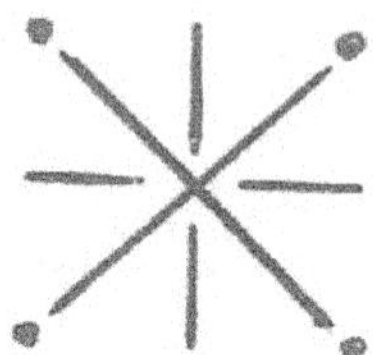

"Where to next?" Ty asked.

Abe pointed with his head. "Over there. I can't wait to show you this." He looked down at her with a big smile.

"What's up?" she said with a look of curiosity on her face.

"Won't tell."

"What?"

"You'll see in a bit. Once I go inside, I'll need to open the shutters so we can see."

"Okay, I'll wait. You know, I feel like I've been here before. Like a Deja Vu kind of thing." As the room lit up, her hands flew up to her mouth with a gasp. "Oh, my!" she said as she limped into the room. "I understand what you mean now." She walked to the spacious countertop at the end of the long room. "This was my room!"

"I'm not surprised," he smiled.

"This wooden countertop sends tingles up my arm," she said as she caressed it. She stood there slowly studying the ancient woodwork that decorated this space.

A huge open space for tables filled part of the room. Shelves with baskets covering each one lined the walls. Abe opened a double door on the far side. Behind it, she saw another wall with more shelves.

She examined one of the baskets. "I need to connect consciously with whatever is here."

Abe knew she needed to acknowledge and respect the energy of the room with her mind.

"Mind to Mind," she reminded herself.

"I need to honor the Spirit of this Apothecary," she said aloud, more to herself than to Abe. "This is no normal Apothecary. I need to respect the guardian here."

"The Mystery School built this building to embody the ancient healing arts for spiritual genetics as well as the physical," Abe told her. "The apothecary was just one aspect of the school, all of which deserves our honor. Align yourself with them."

"May I, Tythea, reconnect with the Spirit of this Apothecary?" As soon as those words came out of her mouth, a brilliant, sparkling green ball of energy appeared in the corner of the room.

Welcome back, mistress, a voice from the energy ball said.

"This was my place, right?" she asked.

Yes, indeed. I have been waiting for your return.

"May I again enter this Sacred Space? May I reconnect with you? And I respectfully ask you to help me to remember what I need to know."

Yes, you may. I will remind you of what you once knew about the ancient ways.

"Thank you, thank you." Ty placed her palms over her heart and bowed out of honor and respect as the vision faded. "It comforts me knowing you are my teacher from long ago."

She sent a conscious wave of energy out through her heart to connect with the wholeness that Zathera embodied.

"Wow," Abe said. I felt that."

"Omni," she whispered. "I love you and all that you represent in me."

She repeated her alignment ritual for the Apothecary. "I understand you give me permission to make a closer inspection of the room's contents." The dim light made it difficult to see. She examined the contents in a covered bin with her hands. This one contained dried leaves, herbs of some kind. She crushed a handful with her fingers. A strong, pungent scent of sage filled the room. "That couldn't have been sitting on the shelf very long. It smells so fresh," she said. "Abe, come and check this out. I found some sage and it is still smells viable."

"What?"

Ty stuck her tongue into the powder. "Try it," she said. "It tastes wonderful."

Abe tasted the crushed sage leaves. "You're right!" he said.

Ty looked over and saw some more bins. "Yep, here is more."

Abe checked another one. "Gosh, I can't believe they are still good after a thousand years. How is that possible? They must have used some secret way of preserving them."

"You know what? I think it's the way everything here is made," Ty replied. "The buildings aren't decaying. Nothing ever dies here. It's suspended in time, in a space of its own. This whole mountain is in a death-free zone."

She picked up one of the herbs to feel its energy. She closed her eyes as it glowed in her palm. "It's still radiant, its energy field still intact. It's as vibrant as if it was just picked. Look for yourself."

"That's incredible," Abe said. "I guess it's just another mystery to solve. It has a different color and a slightly different texture but other than that it looks the same."

"This has to be a little different because of preserving and maintaining the life of the herbs for so long," she surmised.

"You're probably right, but how?"

"The Zibors tell me they help. They carry life to anything that wishes to maintain awareness, which happened with this construction." Ty thanked them for their explanation. "We have every herb we'll ever need right here! And then some" she said. "I don't even know what all of them are. There must be some records around here. I don't know if we could even read them."

"True, it's a bit of a problem. I guess you must trust your intuition. Tune into the ancient part of yourself that knows. You can talk to plants. It might take time, but I know you can figure it out."

"Right. Thanks for reminding me and for pulling me out of feeling overwhelmed. I had a momentary lapse. I needed to get out of my head, to relax and trust my knowledge." She moved to some of the other shelves. She found mortars and pestles of various sizes, everything she needed. "It's still so hard to believe," she said, shaking her head in disbelief. "I have everything here waiting for me."

She suddenly shuddered.

"Are you alright? Abe asked with concern in his voice.

"I think I just collided with my past self. She's still here. It feels weird. I felt a similar energy this morning in the cabin, but I didn't think much of it, then." She stood quietly for a bit. "It was my parallel self. My parents talked about parallels, but I never understood them. This gives me a feel for it. They said it happens when you move into simultaneous time, where everything happens at once. That's a mindblower, Abe! We will remember what we once knew and use it now."

After a few moments, Abe said, "This place still holds everything that ever happened in it. It's a reservoir. It remembers because it's alive, a being made from this earth just like us. We're part of its memory. And the Zibors are part of it as well. They help us to create a bridge to what we once knew, along with Source."

"So," Ty spoke up, "we just need to relax and let the answer come. It's all here to be re-remembered and we will open to it when it's time. I'm feeling a bit overwhelmed. I need to sit and relax."

"Do you want to go into the commons area to rest while I open all the shutters to air out the place? We need to get a breeze moving through all the rooms."

"Yes. We have a lot of cleaning to do at some point."

He picked her up and took her to a covered chair. Underneath the covering, she found a beautifully carved bench with room for several people. "I've never seen anything like it before," she said as she rubbed her hand on the wood. "All we have at home were stools or cushions on the floor." She laid back and put her leg up on the armrest. Her head nodded as she fell asleep. She woke with a start and looked around to see Abe sitting in a chair close by.

"Hi, sleepy head."

"I dozed off, didn't I?" she said, slightly confused.

"Yes, you had a good nap. Do you feel better?"

"Yes, I think so." She lowered her leg and tried to sit up, but found it hard. He came to help. They sat side by side in silence. "I need to upgrade my energy level because I'm still feeling a bit wonky." She paused a moment. "I feel a shift ripple through me. I remember seeing the face of a beautiful woman in my dream," she told Abe. "I'm sure it is my parallel I connected into earlier. Hi," she told her parallel. "Oh, wow! I feel my two parts merging. It's an amazing feeling!" She took several deep breaths. "Wait. There's something else. Of course. That's what I saw in my dream, the experience of running into my past self." She turned to Abe. "All better now. I didn't realize I was so tired."

"Maybe we're pushing things too quickly," he told her. "You probably need more rest before we take this tour."

"I know," she told him in a sad tone. "I'd like to go on, but I'm not sure I can."

"Let's not explore anymore today. But I need to walk you through two areas I think you'll want to see. A quick walk through, and out the back door, okay?"

"OK, I guess I'll have to be satisfied with that for now."

He took her to a door off the commons area. "This you must see." He stopped in front of a big door, and she lifted its lever. Light filled the room as in the commons area. Dust and dirt lay everywhere. A huge indoor 'outhouse,' much like the one in the cabin sat in the corner. The cabinets revealed the same expert workmanship as those in the cabin. "Over there behind that wall are private stools, like ours, and washing bowls." In the middle of the room sat three group bathing pools and places for quick showers. She started to ask a question, but he stopped her. "Hey, no questions, no investigations now, remember?"

"Whoever designed this did an amazing job. I love that it's all inside. I can't wait to have a wonderful, hot bath at some point."

"Yeah, you and me both. Going to the headwaters and going swimming should satisfy us for now."

"So, I assume there are two identical group bathing chambers?"

"Yes, of course."

"Wow, they are huge, aren't they? Where to next?"

"Well, let's see." He started walking towards the door. They turned a corner, and she saw a huge, open room with tables and benches.

"The dining hall," she said.

He walked on through the hall, towards the kitchen beyond the wall. A drop-down wall and a lower counter divided the two rooms. Several cooking hearths and ovens sat along the outside wall on the far side. Overhead, a row of windows that served as a skylight. These differed from the windows in the rest of the building. Gemstones covered parts of the skylight but still let in enough light to send rainbow colors dancing throughout the room. "How did they do that? What is the clear material that allows light to come in? Why in here and not in the other rooms?"

"Don't know," he said. "Another mystery to add to the list."

He led her to the back door. She pulled the lever and swung it open. She saw an outside cooking area for the summertime in addition to the inside kitchen. They crossed a rock patio area and came to a stop at the end of a grass-covered yard.

"You wondered where I got the veggies and fruit I've been gathering, right?"

"Yes."

"It's from out there. Out beyond the grass is the garden that replants itself every year.

"What?"

"Yes, all of this is for us." He turned to the south and showed her the trees covered in fruit. Some were ripe and some not quite so.

"This is incredible!" Ty exclaimed. "I thought it might just be a small area but it's not."

"It's all here waiting for us."

"Wow."

They walked to a tree covered with red fruit from which Ty picked several. She put one in his mouth and a smaller one in hers. "Yum, this is wonderful."

He walked her down a path behind the end of the Hall. Fruit trees covered the entire area. Behind those, she saw another large building.

"What's back there?"

"Storage and another outdoor kitchen where food and herbs can be dried and preserved, and a large cellar. They passed several other buildings before returning to their cabin. Abe noticed how quiet Ty became during their short hike. "Are you okay?" he asked.

"Yes, but no. I know it's a weird answer. I'm okay, but energy-wise I'm not. I'm integrating a lot, and it's zapping me good."

"Energy overdose?"

"Yes. There's a lot to absorb. I think I need to slow down and take a nap again. Is that okay?"

"Sure, it is." I wondered if all this might be pushing you too much. You've been through a lot both physically and spiritually over the last two days.

"Maybe you're right."

"Even with me carrying you, your body probably needs more rest."

"Yes. I was just so excited about being here and wanting to check everything out. I guess, now that I'm here, I need to relax and tell my curiosity to wait. We're not going anywhere. I didn't expect there to be so much. Come to think about it, I didn't truthfully know what to expect."

"I know what you mean," he said. He carried her to her room. "Get some rest and I'll fix us something to eat. Then we'll go swimming if you feel up to it. How does that sound?"

"Great. My body would love that," she said, a surge of joy showing on her face. "Stop here," she said. "I need a privy break."

He went back to the front room and sat down to rest. He performed a quick review of the day. He remembered how going through the buildings for the first time gave him a bit of a shock. *Surely in her depleted state, it must have drained her physically and spiritually.* It took him almost a week to do so, but he hadn't experienced anything like what they had this morning. *What made it so different?* he wondered. *Maybe because we did it together. There is something mighty powerful going on. It must be us as a couple.* He realized he quickly went through all the buildings and didn't take the time to tune into anything. *I just wanted to get a sense of all of this on a mental level.* He knew he would come back later. He saw his reflection in her.

Curiosity drove many of his actions and behaviors. His dad and uncle awakened his inquisitive side. He felt the urge to satisfy this side of himself before he took the time to check out the energetics of the whys and what-fors. He needed to curb that behavior to relax into the spiritual aspect of all of this. He suspected a bit of it came from ego, but he interpreted it as curiosity. Having an inquiring nature pulls you forward in life. He found that it worked for him here. He realized why he needed to do it with her. A couple of structures still called him because he hadn't taken the time to search them, yet. He heard a sort of warning that it wasn't time to search them, so he told himself they would have to wait.

The End

Acknowledgments

I want to thank Joseph, my best friend and partner in life, for his encouragement and support as I learned to walk this out in me. His knowledge guided me as I learned to live in this reality, which felt so strange to me, not like my original home. Many of you may feel the same way. I want to thank my daughter, Rocksye, for being my best student and teacher as she's learned to apply these practices in her body energy work. Thanks to the many close family members and friends who've grounded these new understandings by taking them to heart and allowing them to blossom in the garden of their soul. Their daily practice has allowed them to reclaim their own power. This achievement establishes a grid for the foundation of new teachings about a deeper inner life on earth. Thanks to my editors, Joseph and Wayne, and to my publisher, Amy at Quill Hawk, without whom none of this would be possible.

The first books that truly spoke to my heart essence with deeper understandings were a series called *Right Use of Will* by Ceanne DeRohan and *Joy Riding the Universe*, and related material, by Sheridon Bryce. They helped me to understand my strange Immaculate Conception, which began a process that changed me to my core. I gradually evolved out of the old Adam and Eve matrix of separation into a new template that gave birth to the Divine within. Buried within my story are the codes that will transform our present genetics. They, indeed, led me on an unusual voyage of self-discovery, resurrecting parts of my soul that I had forgotten. Our mission, dear reader, is to reopen this closed door and live in a body that is fully self-conscious.

About the Author

Shoena Helen Harris was born into a large family on a religious commune in the Ozarks of southern Missouri. She survived a premature birth after her mother was accidentally injured. The second of eight children, under the stern rule of her grandfather, the members were kept isolated from the influences of modern American culture. At an early age, the children learned to work alongside the adults to raise all their food. Nevertheless, they had a large group of playmates to enjoy the wilderness around them when free to do so. From as far back as she could remember, unique spiritual experiences had been breaking into her life. Destiny started calling.

At the age of sixteen, a stranger came calling. He asked her to marry him. Shortly afterwards, he was asked to leave, and she went with him to begin her next phase of education as wife, mother, and worker. A series of books, called *The Right Use of Will*, came to her attention, which began her independent spiritual training. Sometime later, her husband passed away, her daughter married, and she was left to start a new life of self-discovery. Hidden within this story are some of the experiences and lessons she learned in this new life that led her into new forms of artistry and creativity, blossoming further with each new day. This book marks the beginning of her effort to share with readers the depths of the love and understanding she has received through her multidimensional inner journeys.

www.ingramcontent.com/pod-product-compliance
Lightning Source LLC
Chambersburg PA
CBHW070455300726
48975CB00007B/2184